Lydia

BRIDES OF THE OREGON TRAIL
BOOK TWO

CYNTHIA WOOLF

LYDIA

ISBN-13: 978-1-947075-92-4

LYDIA is a work of fiction. Names, characters, places, brands, media and incidents either are the product of the author's imagination or are used fictitiously. Any resemblance to actual persons, living or dead, events, or locales, is entirely coincidental.

Published by Firehouse Publishing
Interior formatting: Author E.M.S.

Books written by Cynthia Woolf can be obtained either through the author's official website or through select, online book retailers.

www.cynthiawoolf.com

Books by Cynthia Woolf

Brides of the Oregon Trail
Hannah
Lydia

Brides of Seattle
Mail Order Mystery
Mail Order Mayhem
Mail Order Mix-Up
Mail Order Moonlight
Mail Order Melody

Central City Brides
The Dancing Bride
The Sapphire Bride
The Irish Bride
The Pretender Bride

Montana Sky World
A Family for Christmas
Kissed by a Stranger
Thorpe's Mail-Order Bride

Hope's Crossing
The Hunter Bride
The Replacement Bride
The Stolen Bride
The Unexpected Bride

American Mail-Order Brides
Genevieve, Bride of Nevada

The Surprise Brides

Gideon

The Brides of Tombstone

Mail Order Outlaw

Mail Order Doctor

Mail Order Baron

The Brides of San Francisco

Nellie

Annie

Cora

Sophia

Amelia

Destiny in Deadwood

Jake

Liam

Zach

Matchmaker & Co.

Capital Bride

Heiress Bride

Fiery Bride

Colorado Bride

The Tame Series

Tame a Wild Heart

Tame a Wild Wind

Tame a Wild Bride

Tame a Honeymoon Heart

Box Sets

Destiny in Deadwood: The Complete Series

The Tame Series

CHAPTER 1

November 16, 1852

Lydia climbed out of the wagon and looked up, thankful to see the sun shining bright. Perhaps the walk to town wouldn't be as bad today as it was yesterday. She walked into town from the outskirts where the wagon train stopped.

More than happy to be wearing her best dress and not the ragged skirts and dresses she'd worn for the last six and a half months, she didn't mind the walk. She held her skirt high so as not to get it muddy until she reached town. There she certainly didn't mind walking on the wood planks of the boardwalk instead of rough roads, full of ruts from previous wagons and either dry and dusty or slick with mud.

The wagon train stood on the east side of town. With the rainy weather they'd had since arriving two days ago, she still wore her boots, refusing to ruin her good shoes in this muck.

Passing the butcher, the general store and the bank she made her way to the sheriff's office. People passed her and she probably should have asked them about Walter, but she didn't want anyone to know her business. Instead, she'd waited for two days for Walter to show up at the wagon train so they could marry and start their life together.

Figuring something was wrong, perhaps that he was sick, she decided to check with the Oregon City sheriff. Naturally, his office was at the side of town opposite from the wagons. Finally reaching his office she knocked once and then entered.

Behind the average wooden desk was a man in his late thirties, with dark blond hair and arresting light green eyes. He wore a plaid flannel shirt with a black wool vest with a five point star badge pinned to the vest.

"What can I do for you, Miss…?"

"Granger. Lydia Granger. You can help me by directing me to the home of Mr. Walter Mosley. I am Mr. Mosley's fiancée and he was supposed to come and claim me, for lack of a better word, and we were to marry."

He stood immediately upon hearing her name. "Miss Granger, I've been waiting for you. My name is Robert McCauley. Walt was my dearest friend. You never met anyone kinder than Walt Mosley."

Lydia's stomach started to tighten. She cocked her head just a bit to the left and narrowed her eyes. "Was? Did you have a falling out?" She began to chew her lip, hoping that reason was the case, because she didn't like the other possibility at all.

He shook his head. "No, ma'am. I'm very sorry to say, Walt passed away three weeks ago. Doc said it was a heart attack. Walt left you something though. He said if he passed we should read it together."

"Passed? He can't be dead." Lydia swayed. *This can't be happening. What will I do now? Without Walter I have nothing and no one. Hannah has Joe. She'll be fine, but what will I do without Walter?*

The sheriff moved quickly and held her by the shoulders. "Here, sit." He helped her to the ladder-backed chair in front of his desk. "Are you better?"

"Yes. It's just such a shock." She looked down at her lap. "I don't know what to do now. I...I'm sorry." Taking a handkerchief from her reticule, she dabbed at her eyes. "It's just that for the past year and a half, I've planned on marrying Walter Mosley and now I simply don't know what I'll do."

"Let's read his will. You'll have a better grasp of things afterward."

The sheriff handed her an envelope and then leaned against the desk while she read the contents.

The envelope contained a single sheet of paper.

I, Walter Augustus Mosley, being of sound mind and body, do hereby leave all my assets and worldly goods to my fiancée, Miss Lydia Granger. Signed Walter A. Mosley, March 7, 1852

The combination to the safe is 12 right, 17 left, two spins to 52 right, and three spins to 23 left.

She recognized the handwriting. It was the same as in his letters. Lydia looked at the sheriff. "Is this document legal?"

"Yes, ma'am. You can see from the signatures at the bottom that Mr. Elmer Fulton and myself were witnesses. Walt trusted me with it and bade me to give it to you when you arrived, if he couldn't be here to meet you. He never doubted you would come."

She lifted her brows and her eyes widened. "Of course, I came. I gave him my word and he seemed like such a nice man." *Walt trusted me, believed in me, I knew he was a good man.*

The sheriff nodded and looked out the window.

It almost seemed like he was seeing his old friend.

"He was a good man and my best friend. He helped this community very much."

Lydia put her hand to her throat. "I hope to make Walter proud of me and to follow in his footsteps. Although I'm feeling a bit overwhelmed at the moment, I want to make Oregon City my home."

"I'm very glad to hear that."

"Um, I don't mean to be disrespectful, but I assume since there is a safe, a house must be around it?"

Robert chuckled. "Yes, Miss Granger. Let me take you to your new home." He opened the top drawer of his desk and withdrew two keys wired together, which he put in his vest pocket. Then he grabbed his hat from the peg by the door and donned it before opening the door. He waved his arm out in front of him. "After you."

They walked two blocks toward the west and then three blocks north. The people they met all greeted the sheriff with smiles. They passed several nice little houses that Lydia would have loved to have. Cottages, with nice little gardens out front.

When they finally stopped it was in front of one of the largest houses Lydia had ever seen, not only here but in Independence as well. The two-story home was sided with wood, but stone went halfway up the first floor and was used for the three chimneys. Painted light blue with white shutters and trim, with a white picket fence around the front yard, the house was quite charming despite its size. Four steps led to the wide porch which ran the length of the front of the house. She saw a swing on one side of the door and a table and four chairs on the other.

Lydia put a hand to her throat. "Oh, my, I..." She swallowed hard. "I never expected something like this place. Mr. Mosley, Walter, said he was well off, but I assumed that status still meant something more...shall we say modest." *This house means security for me and Hannah and Joe. We'll never have to worry about getting evicted like we were in Independence or being homeless like we were when Mother and Daddy died.*

"You'll find Walt spared no expense in his home or its furnishings. He was poor as a boy and vowed, when he grew up, he'd live better than all the rich people in his home country of England."

On shaky legs, Lydia walked to the swing and slumped into it, resting her elbows on her knees. "What kind of fiancée was I? I didn't even know he was English."

Robert leaned against the railing. "He never advertised the fact, other than his accent which he couldn't hide, and he only nodded when someone mentioned it. As far as he was concerned, he was American, through and through."

She ran her hand along the beautiful, carved wood of the swing. She'd never seen anything like it. She stood. "Well, I guess you'd better show me the rest of the house. Then I have to get my sister and her husband. They simply will not believe this news."

He waved an arm toward the door. "Yes, ma'am, this way." Taking keys out of his pocket, he unlocked the door and then handed her the keys. "This is for you."

Lydia looked down at the simple iron keys lying in her hand and slowly closed her fingers around them. Blinking back tears, she gazed skyward.

"Thank you, Walter. I'll make you proud you trusted me to carry on for you."

Sheriff McCauley opened the door wide and held it for her.

She stepped through into a different world. The floors were hardwood and covered with Persian carpets, just like the ones in the Ritz Hotel in Independence. These were in shades of blue with different motifs of paisley or stars and some designs she didn't recognize.

To her right was a formal living room. The room was large, the sofa and two Queen Anne chairs upholstered in maroon with gold accents. A low table sat between them with the configuration of the furniture close enough to allow intimate discussions.

Bookshelves covered one wall. Large windows took up most of two more walls, with the French entry door to the hallway on the fourth.

To her left just down the hall, was a formal dining room. She'd never lived in a house with a separate dining room. They'd eaten in the kitchen at a plain pine table. The table and chairs, enough to seat twenty, were built from dark cherry wood. She'd recognize that wood anywhere because her mother had always admired the set in the window of Lewellyn Brothers Furniture in downtown Independence. Hanging above the table was a beautiful crystal chandelier. *Owly will love it for his perch.*

"I assume the kitchen is in the rear of the house?"

"Yes, the kitchen and the bath. He had a room built with a small stove to heat water for the bathtub."

Lydia clapped her hands once. "Oh, how wonderful. That will be so much more convenient and allow for privacy whereas a tub in the middle of the kitchen like we had in Independence allowed for neither."

"Yes, ma'am."

"Please, stop calling me ma'am. I'm just twenty-one and hardly a ma'am. Call me Lydia, and I'll call you Robert. Agreed?" She held out a hand.

Smiling, he reached out and shook her hand. "Agreed…Lydia. I'll let you explore the rest of the house at your leisure. I must return to work."

"I'm sure my brother-in-law has talked to you already. He's Joe Stanton, the bounty hunter. Some of the fugitives he was chasing were on the wagon train."

He tipped his hat. "He has. He didn't mention you though. If you need anything, you know where to find me. Good day, Miss…er…Lydia."

She ducked her head. "Good day, Robert. Oh, I would like to know where Walter is buried. I will want to pay my respects."

"I'll write down the directions and send them to you with one of my deputies."

"Thank you."

Lydia wanted to go through the house, but felt strange doing it alone. She'd get Hannah and Joe, maybe they could dispel the eerie feeling she had about the house.

Lydia locked her new home and walked to the wagon train to share the news with Hannah and Joe. The three of them were still living in the wagon, though now much of the items in the wagon were unloaded to make room to sleep. Or they had just been used up as was the case of the bags of flour, sugar and cornmeal.

Hannah was as pale as Joe was dark. She had porcelain skin that was barely tanned, even after the hard journey here from Missouri. And now she had a glow about her that only being pregnant could explain. Her red hair had lightened a little from the short time she left it uncovered in the sun. Both she and Lydia had religiously worn their bonnets, shading their faces from the sun. Not only was a sunburn bad for the skin, it was painful as well.

Joe, on the other hand, was very tan and his blue eyes were striking against his brown skin. She smiled and shook her head. He still needed a haircut. His hair hung below his shoulders now, black as coal.

Standing six feet three inches tall, he towered a good eight inches over Hannah and was more than a foot taller than Lydia. But he was one of the kindest men she'd ever met and, more importantly, he loved Hannah completely. She'd never seen her sister so happy.

The November weather in Oregon City had been rainy and cold, but the temperature rose enough so that Lydia took off her cloak and sat on one of the chairs she'd gotten out for their last night on the trail. Prior to that they'd used buckets to sit on. Having used them for six months was more than enough. If she'd been smart, she'd have gotten the chairs out sooner, but retying them every night didn't appeal to her.

"Walter is dead." Her voice broke as the enormity of the situation washed over her. "He died three weeks ago."

Hannah embraced her. "Oh, Lydie. I'm so sorry."

Lydia shook her head. "Walter is still looking out for me."

Joe leaned against the wagon. "What do you mean?"

"Well…you'll never believe this…I still don't believe it. He left everything to me in his will."

Hannah's emerald green eyes widened in surprise. "You're funning us, right?

"I'm not." She held up the keys Robert gave her. "Now, would you both come with me and look over the place you'll live until you get your home built?"

Joe straightened and joined the women near the fire. "Are you sure you want us living there?"

"Of course," replied Lydia. "You're my family and you'll always be welcome in my home. Besides I'd rattle around in that house if it was just me alone with my babies."

"And you will always be welcome in ours, too," said Hannah. "Once it's built."

Lydia donned her cloak again. "So let's go. It will be faster if we ride your horses. I can ride with Hannah."

Hannah shook her head. "You best ride with Joe. I haven't ridden with anyone else and don't trust my skills yet."

Lydia gazed over at Joe. "So brother-in-law, will you take me home?"

"Of course. But better yet. Let's just take the wagon to the house. Then you'll have your babies with you, too."

"That's a good idea. Thanks, Joe."

He walked over and gave her a hug. "What else are brothers good for?"

Lydia laughed. "Many things. Many, many things."

Joe had his horse tied to the back of the wagon and the oxen harnessed and ready to go in about twenty minutes. Hannah rode her horse while Joe drove the wagon with Lydia.

They went to the Mosley home, parked the wagon and tied the horses to the hitching rail.

"Let's leave the animals out here for now. I haven't looked upstairs yet. If it's anything like down here, the rooms will be magnificent."

Hannah and Joe both stood looking at the house with their mouths open.

Knowing exactly how they felt, Lydia smiled. "Come on," she said, breaking their trance.

"My gosh, Lydie, this house is amazing." Hannah stood hand to her throat, staring at the house.

"I know. Come look." Lydia opened the door and pocketed the keys. "There's a safe which I haven't opened yet. I'm not even sure where it is. I've only seen the front rooms."

They gave cursory looks to the living and dining rooms then went down the hall on the right side of the stairs, past the living room to the library.

Lydia couldn't believe the house held more books. Bookshelves stood from floor to ceiling on every wall that wasn't window, even around the door. And all were nearly full of books. The writer in her was thrilled to have so much to read. Mixed in with the books were pieces of art, vases, plates, masks. The whole room was amazing, but what dominated the room was the huge safe behind the large desk.

She pulled the will from her reticule, walked to the safe and followed the instructions for the combination, grabbing the handle afterward. Nothing.

"I must have done something wrong." She held up her hands and they were shaking. "I'm nervous. Let me try this again."

The second time supplied the same results as the first.

"Doggone it. Why can't I open this?" She hit the door with her fist.

"Here Lydia, let me." Joe held his hand out for the paper. He followed the combination, the handle lifted and he pulled open the safe.

Lydia frowned. "How'd you do that? I followed the instructions to the letter."

"I bet you missed one of the spins. It's an unusual combination to have three spins before the number."

"Oh," she gritted her teeth and then sighed. "I thought the number was on the third spin."

Joe chuckled. "An easy mistake to make."

Lydia's jaw dropped. She looked at Hannah and Joe. They each stood with the same amazed expression she knew she wore. Inside the safe, stacks of cash were on the bottom and jewelry boxes on the middle shelves, and what looked like a set of bookkeeping books and other papers on the top shelf.

She shook her head slowly. "I don't know what to do first…open the jewelry boxes or count the money. I have to make an inventory so I know what I have inherited."

Then the thought hit her and she was filled with joy. She could take care of her animals the way they should be taken care of. Now she could buy the meat her wolf pup, Sampson, and puma cub, Simba, needed without wondering where she'd find the money. She no longer needed to rely on Joe to hunt for her in order to feed them properly.

She looked up and murmured, "Thank you, Walter Mosley."

Hannah nodded. "You do need to make an inventory."

From the desk, Lydia found paper, pen and ink.

"We'll help. Let's do the jewelry first. You can make a list as we open them."

Hannah and Joe each took a few jewelry boxes. They took turns. First Hannah opened a box, called out its contents and placed it on the desk. Then Joe did the same and they took turns.

"This one has a sapphire necklace and ear bobs," said Joe.

Hannah whistled. "Oh, my. Here is a large diamond ring. I bet this is your engagement ring. Why don't you try it on?"

Lydia shook her head. "Oh, I couldn't." *How can I wear a ring from Walter that he didn't put on my finger? I'm surprised that I feel grief for a man I never met, but I do wish he wasn't dead. I wish we were getting married and starting our life together.*

"Why not?" Hannah waved at all the boxes of gems. "These are all yours now. You might as well wear them."

Lydia took the ring from her sister. The fit was a little small, but she pushed it on. "This isn't coming off without a little grease."

They opened the rest of the boxes to reveal a wedding band encircled with diamonds, a diamond necklace set, a ruby set and an emerald set. Each one had an incredible necklace and tasteful ear bobs. Several smaller boxes also contained sets of diamond cufflinks and tie tacks, as well as emerald, ruby and sapphire sets. Lastly, he had five gorgeous gold pocket watches. *Joe would probably like one of those.*

Lydia suddenly wondered who helped Walter pick out all of the jewelry, furniture and artwork. Had he selected them himself? She supposed, given his wealth, he could have taken the time to learn about the art and the other items.

Was she actually feeling jealous that she didn't get to make the decisions with him? She was even sorrier she'd never met him. He seemed knowledgeable, educated and could have taught her things. Maybe they could have taught each other things. She didn't know what exactly, but she wished she'd have gotten to find out.

"Shall we count the money now?" asked Lydia.

"With the way it's wrapped and stacked, that shouldn't take as long as you might think," said Joe. "Each pack of twenty-dollar bills contains one thousand dollars. Each stack contains twenty packs of bills and you have..." He stopped and counted, pulling the packs of bills out as he went. "Twenty-two stacks of bills. That's four-hundred and forty thousand dollars. Good grief, Lydia, you need to hire armed guards. What the heck did Walter do to make this much money?"

"He told me he made it in the California gold fields."

Lydia sat in the desk chair before her legs collapsed under her. "Four-hundred-thousand dollars. Do you know what this means? Walter was rich. Not just well off, but filthy stinking rich."

She looked over at Joe. "Do you really believe we should hire guards? It doesn't appear Walter had them. As long as I don't go around talking about the money I have at home, I should be fine, shouldn't I? I do wonder why he had so much cash at home instead of the bank. It appears that for some reason, Walter didn't trust the bank to safeguard his money."

Joe put the cash back in the safe.

Hannah put the jewels in.

Lydia stopped her, lifted one of the boxes and handed it to her sister. "You should take the emeralds. They match your eyes and will look fabulous with your bright red hair and pale skin."

"I couldn't." Hannah, eyes shining, looked at Joe.

He smiled. "I don't know why not. She's right they will look great on you."

"Don't think I've forgotten you, Joe. Take the matching emerald cufflinks and a tie bar plus one or two of the beautiful pocket watches. Both of you take what you like."

"Thank you, Lydia. That's very generous of you," said Joe.

"Nonsense. You're my family, my only family. I just can't believe Walter would have all this here but for whatever reason, it is all of ours."

"Thank you, Lydie. I think we'd best keep these items in the safe until we need them." Hannah put her box back on the middle shelf. She reached out to Joe and he placed his items in her hand. She added those to the treasures in the safe.

Lydia clapped her hands once and then grinned. "Shall we go look at the rest of the house? I'm dying to see the kitchen. After cooking for the last six months over a camp fire, I wonder if I still know how to cook on a stove."

"Well, I guess you'll find out shortly," Hannah said. "I assume you're fixing supper tonight."

"Yes, but that depends on what's in the larder. If it's empty, as I suspect, I'll have to go shopping before I can prepare a meal."

Hannah hooked her arm through Lydia's. "Well, let's go find out, shall we?"

Entering the kitchen, Lydia took three steps into the room and came to a dead stop.

"Will you look at that? Have you ever seen anything so beautiful? A four-burner stove, with green porcelain doors on the oven, warming rack, and fire door." *This will be so much fun to cook on. I can't wait.*

Hannah put her hands on Lydia's shoulders. "Oh, my. This whole room is lovely. Look at the cupboards, the table and chairs, they all match. They look like they're what...oak...maybe. This house is not just bigger but also so much nicer than our rented room in Independence."

Lydia spread her arms and turned in a circle smiling. "All I know is I can't wait to fix a meal."

She found the bathing room the sheriff told her about and there was a bedroom behind the kitchen for the help if they ever hired someone.

A knock sounded on the front door.

Cocking her head, Lydia stopped. "I wasn't expecting anyone and the only person who knows I'm here is the sheriff. Maybe he's thought of something else he needs to tell me."

"We'll come with you," said Joe. "Just in case."

They walked across the house and Joe stood next to Lydia as she opened the door.

"May I help you?"

A handsome man with brown hair curling a little over his collar and nice brown eyes stood on the porch. He was as tall as Joe, at least six feet, three inches, which meant he towered over Lydia's five feet four inches.

"Lydia Granger?"

She frowned and her hand clamped tighter around the knob. *How does he know my name?* She looked up at him, an eyebrow raised. "Yes. How can I help you, sir?"

"I'm hoping we can help each other. I have reason to believe Walter Mosley was murdered."

CHAPTER 2

Her stomach did somersaults and she narrowed her eyes, frowning. "Murdered? I don't know what you mean, sir. Please explain yourself."

"May I come in?"

She shook her head. "No. I don't even know who you are."

Joe stepped in front of her, his gun in his hand and pointed the weapon at the stranger on the porch. "Do you want me to get rid of this man for you?"

"Wait." The man put up his hands. "Please. Let me explain. My name is Max Caldwell. I'm a detective with the Walsh Detective Agency out of Chicago. Up until 1848, when they disbanded, I was a Texas Ranger. I have information about your inheritance. Specifically the money held at the Oregon City Bank."

Walter had money in the bank, too? But why have it there and so much here? If this man was right and Walter was murdered, I owe it to him to discover who and how.

She reached over and placed a hand on top of Joe's. "Let's hear what the man has to say. Come in Mr. Caldwell."

With Hannah behind them she and Joe both stepped back to allow the stranger entry.

Lydia grabbed Hannah's hand. "Follow us, please." She led him into the living room and waved at one of the armchairs, before seating herself on the sofa.

Hannah settled next to her.

Joe sat on the arm of the couch next to Hannah.

Mr. Caldwell sat in the chair Lydia indicated, across from the sofa.

"Now, please explain yourself," said Lydia. "You said you suspect my fiancé was murdered."

"I've been on the trail of the man called Horace Belcher for nearly two years. He's the president of the Oregon City Bank, where Walter Mosley lived, and now you are, the largest depositor."

"I know little about the bank account, but what does that have to do with Walter's murder? Why have you been trailing this," she waved a hand in front of her,"Horace Belcher?"

He leaned forward and looked directly into Lydia's eyes. "Because his name is really, Gilbert Ross. He's wanted for the murder of the *real* Horace Belcher, back in Chicago."

"What does this have to do with Walter's death? You said you thought he was murdered. Why? How?" asked Lydia.

"I believe he was poisoned. Horace Belcher, the bank president and the man I'm after was the last to see Walter alive. According to a very talkative clerk at the hotel, Belcher took tea with Walter, here in this house, the same day he died. It was Belcher who reported the death to Sheriff McCauley."

"And because he was the last to see him alive you think he killed him? That seems a bit of a stretch."

"You don't know him like I do. There is also a rumor, according to the clerk, that Walter was about to fire Belcher. That gives him motive. The afternoon tea may have been the time of the actual firing, but regardless it gave him opportunity."

"That seems like a lot of hearsay to base your opinion of this man's guilt upon, but I do want to get to the bottom of Walter's death, whether it was from natural causes or something more sinister. So how can I help you?" Lydia asked.

"More importantly, why should she help you?" asked Hannah.

"That's a fair question, Miss—"

"Mrs. Stanton. I'm Hannah," she raised her hand toward Joe next to her. "This is my husband, Joe. I'm Lydia's sister."

Caldwell stood and extended his hand to Joe and then to Hannah before sitting again. "I'm pleased to meet you. I've heard of you, Mr. Stanton. You're quite successful in your field."

"Thank you," said Joe. "Now, just what do you want from Lydia?"

Mr. Caldwell smiled, revealing straight white teeth beneath firm, full lips. *What's the matter with me? Why am I thinking about his lips?*

Max leaned back in the chair and crossed his ankle over his knee, resting his hat on the circle formed from the movement. He stared hard at Lydia. "It's really very simple. I want you to go to the bank, introduce yourself to Belcher and then tell him you want to withdraw all of your money."

Lydia's eyes widened and her brows shot up. "Why on earth would I do that? I have more cash than I can spend right here."

"Lydia!" said Joe.

She looked at him and frowned.

Joe rolled his eyes and slowly shook his head. "You don't go around telling people that. You're just asking to be robbed."

She waved away his comments. "I doubt this man is planning on robbing me. Are you, Mr. Caldwell?"

Max shook his head. "I must agree with your brother-in-law. You can't let people know how much cash you have in that safe. You're putting yourself in danger. There are people here who would as soon kill you for the money in your reticule as look at you."

She crossed her arms over her bosom and narrowed her eyes. "How do you know about the safe? We never mentioned it."

Max suddenly looked guilty. "I broke into the house to see if I could find any proof that would put Belcher away for theft, if not murder. I didn't find any. Nevertheless you put yourself in danger if you talk about the money, in the house, whether in the safe or not."

She lifted a brow. "But what you're suggesting I do, that action won't put me in any kind of danger? Really? Do you expect me to believe that? For some reason, you need Belcher to fear losing access to my money and to make a move concerning my money. Please explain your plan, so I understand what you are really asking of me."

Why am I thinking of him as Max?

Max took a deep breath. "Very well. I'm hoping your request will send him into a panic. He won't have access to your money any longer and you'll find out he's been embezzling from you, which I believe he has. I want him to leave Oregon City, with as much of your money as he can. I'll arrest him for theft and then will hopefully discover the evidence I need to prove he murdered the real Belcher."

"Wait a minute." Joe waved his hands and shook his head. "You want her to make this withdrawal for you and you don't even know what you're looking for? That's ridiculous and very dangerous. Belcher could decide to take her or worse, kill her, to keep her silent. If you're right, he's already killed before, what would keep him from doing it again?"

Lydia looked down in her lap. Her hands lay clasped together, so no one would see them shake.

Max frowned. "It is definitely not without risk but I thought—"

Joe narrowed his eyes and lifted one brow. "You thought since you didn't know my sister-in-law, you would just set her up and too bad if she was injured or killed."

Max stood. "That's not true. I believe I can protect her, but perhaps in my zeal to catch Belcher, I haven't thought this through."

"Please sit, Mr. Caldwell," said Lydia, nodding toward the chair he'd just vacated.

He stayed standing, staring at Joe, with his hands fisted.

Knowing that when dealing with agitated animals, a soothing touch often calms them, Lydia reached over and touched his hand. "Max. Max."

He didn't look at her, but answered. "What?"

"Please. Sit, Max. Let's talk." Why on earth she was feeling so accommodating of this man, she had no idea. Something about him called to her.

He gazed down at her. "I…I'm very sorry, Miss Granger. I'll take my leave now."

Max headed to the door.

Hot on his heels, Lydia said, "Mr. Caldwell… Max…would you come to dinner tonight? I'd like to talk to you." She turned and frowned at Hannah and Joe, irritated at their interference. "Alone, if you're amenable."

He squeezed the hat in his hand and then smiled.

Really smiled, not just gritted his teeth together.

"I'd love to, Miss Granger."

She returned his smile. "I'm Lydia. If I can call you Max, you can surely call me Lydia."

He chuckled. "I guess that situation would be less awkward. Until tonight." He put out his hand and when Lydia placed her hand in his, he brought it to his lips.

Max donned his hat. Before reaching the front door, he stopped, turned and winked at Lydia. Then he left the house.

Hannah placed her hand on Lydia's shoulder. "Lydie, don't let his good looks influence you. What he's asking could be very dangerous. You could easily be killed by this man Belcher."

Lydia looked from Hannah to Joe and then lifted an eyebrow. "I'm well aware of how dangerous it could be. That's why Joe will teach me how to shoot a gun."

The security I was looking forward to with Walt is now gone. I have to learn to take care of myself. Learning to shoot is the first step in that direction.

"I won't," said Joe, crossing his arms over his chest. "That act would be like throwing a torch in the shed full of barrels of black powder."

Lydia mimicked Joe and crossed her arms over her chest. "Then I'll ask Max. Surely given the situation, he'll agree to my request." *He'd better because I'm not going into this situation without being able to protect myself if I need to.*

Joe shook his head. "He's a lawman. He knows better than to arm a...a..."

Hannah slammed her hands to her hips. "If you say arm a woman, you're sleeping in the wagon instead of one of these bedrooms, which we have yet to see. Instead of my strangling you, let's finish looking at the house and then Lydia can go to the mercantile to get the food for her dinner with Mr. Caldwell."

"I take it that means, we're not invited," said Joe.

"You are correct." Lydia lifted her chin, just a bit. "I want this dinner to be business. *My* business with Max. Once I find out more about this situation, maybe I'll help him, maybe I won't, but I'm not making a decision without more information. I don't want a murderer to go free if I can help prevent it. I also don't want to put myself in danger. I have too many lives depending on me."

Max smiled as he walked toward town. Lydia was quite a woman. Much prettier and *younger* than he'd expected. Her beauty, with her blonde hair, the color of corn silk and her blue eyes, startled him. So much so he'd become tongue tied and hadn't presented his case very well at all. What was the matter with him? He'd been around plenty of pretty women and besides, she was much too young for him. He was thirty-four after all.

Thinking about his attraction to Lydia made him remember another reason he was in Oregon City. Yes, he was here as much for his late wife Anna and three-year-old daughter Julia, as for the real Horace Belcher. Belcher had killed Anna when he was escaping. His carriage had hit and killed her as she crossed the street.

Now he had to convince the beautiful Miss Lydia Granger, to put her life on the line. He wanted justice, wanted him tried and punished. If that meant the gallows, all the better.

He headed to his room at the Oregon City Hotel to get cleaned up. It was time he ordered a bath. He'd been here for two weeks and had yet to take the time for a full bath. Now was the time to make a good impression if he expected Miss Granger to help him. And above all else he needed her help.

While Lydia went to the mercantile, Joe and Hannah had brought in Lydia's clothes and other personal belongings and put them away in her room. She'd chosen what she was sure used to be Walter's room. The bed was huge and covered in a quilt that matched the curtains…a silver paisley design on midnight blue background.

All the furniture was heavy, masculine. The bureau, a tall boy chest of drawers, two nightstands, and the table between the two Queen Anne chairs in front of the window were dark cherry. The chairs, positioned perfectly for reading, were upholstered in blue silk. She ran her hand over the material, its texture smooth under her fingertips.

In the corner of the room was a gorgeous Chinese folding screen. She walked over and saw that the chamber pot was hidden behind it.

Opulent was the only word she could think of to describe the room.

Either Walter had been thinking of her or he was careful with his wardrobe because a full-length cheval mirror stood in the corner next to the large closet, which was a room in itself.

Her three dresses looked quite pitiful next to Walter's beautiful suits in shades of white, gray, black, navy blue, and brown. He had about a dozen white shirts and ties that matched each suit, as well as colored shirts of just about every hue. She saw four pairs of different style of boots and six pair of regular men's shoes, in black and white, solid black, brown, gray and white.

She could tell Walter spared no expense when it came to his clothes and he obviously liked clothes and having options.

She emptied the top right drawer in the bureau, combining those clothes with the second drawer and put her under clothes in it. One drawer and it wasn't even full. A pair of bloomers, a chemise, a corset she'd never worn and two nightgowns didn't take up a lot of space. Add in three pairs of socks and two pair of stockings and the drawer still wasn't full.

Lydia shoved the drawer closed, a little too hard. The slam of wood on wood made her suddenly ashamed of her envious thoughts. Walter had left her his money, bless him, and if she wanted to she could buy any dress, coat, shoes or corset she wanted. But that wasn't the person she was. She was frugal, regardless of how much money she had, except where her family was concerned.

She could buy Hannah and Joe whatever they wanted. Again warmth filled her and she was so grateful to Walter Mosley, her guardian angel.

There was a knock at the front door.

She hurried downstairs to answer it.

Lydia opened the door and there was Joe and Hannah with her pets, finally bringing the poor creatures inside and out of the wagon parked in front of the house. Lydia had rigged the wagon with string winding it back and forth in the back and front to form a sort of cage so the little ones wouldn't follow her.

Joe held Sampson, her wolf pup, on a leash with a rope tied loosely around his neck with one hand and in the other arm he held Simba the puma cub.

Hannah held Trinity, the three-legged kitten with one arm and Owly sat on the other arm.

As soon as they came inside and Lydia shut the door behind them, Hannah and Joe, released the animals. They immediately surrounded Lydia, each one vying for attention. She knelt talking to and loving on each one.

Hannah took Owly to the dining room and when she returned to the living room, her face was glowing.

"He made it. He flew to the chandelier. He flapped his little wings and flew unsteadily but he made it and perched on an arm of the light fixture." She grinned and clapped her hands a couple of times. "So did you ever look in the bedrooms?" asked Hannah.

"Just Walter's room. That's where I'm sleeping. You two can choose whatever room you want. Just let me know."

"Thanks for letting us stay. We'll only be here a couple of nights," said Joe. "I filed for my land grant when we left here, before getting the animals from the wagon. The map we have shows it being about ten miles south of town."

Hannah wrapped an arm around Joe's waist. "That's right. As soon as we get supplies tomorrow or the next day we'll be leaving for the land. We have to get a cabin built before winter arrives in full force. Otherwise we'll be living here with you."

"You know you are more than welcome. As a matter of fact, you should probably live here until the baby comes." Lydia dipped her head toward the baby in Hannah's body. "Maybe you can go out for a few days, while the weather is still nice, and then come back when the weather changes for the worst."

Lydia walked to the coat tree near the door. She tossed her black wool crocheted shawl over her shoulders.

"I'll be back in a little while. I need to get groceries for dinner and meat for the animals."

"Do you want help?" asked Hannah.

"No. Then you can check out the other bedrooms and tell me which one you want."

"All right."

"You can also watch the animals. I'm sure they are feeling pretty rambunctious after being caged in the wagon before you rescued them. If you wouldn't mind taking them to the kitchen and keeping them there that would be very helpful."

"They were definitely ready to leave." Hannah smiled. "All except Owly who wasn't happy about leaving his perch and going outside."

"Maybe that's why he flew onto the chandelier so easily," said Lydia.

"That's entirely likely," said Joe.

Sampson barked and put his front paws on Joe's chest and licked his face.

Joe made faces and pushed him down.

"You know, he's getting too big to do that anymore," he said to Lydia.

"Not yet. I still love his kisses. Here, Sampson," called Lydia as she knelt on the floor.

The wolf turned and ran to Lydia. He skidded to a stop just in front of her on the hardwood floor. Then he licked her face. She giggled and petted him, ruffled his neck with both her hands and kissed his nose. The cats, not to be left out, ran to her.

Three-legged Trinity meowed and rubbed against her thigh.

Simba's combination of growling and hissing came out as a sort of weird gutteral sound, reminding her that the three-month-old mountain lion cub was still a baby even though he was huge compared to housecat Trinity.

Lydia stood. "Okay, I need to buy food for these guys. Will you watch them this first time anyway? They need to get used to me leaving and not following."

"Of course," said Hannah. "We'll go pick out our room after putting them in the kitchen so they can't damage any of the furniture or anything else for that matter."

Lydia slipped out the door while Hannah, Joe and all the animals headed to the kitchen.

As she walked into town, Lydia wondered what Max would say when she told him she'd do what he asked.

Chapter 3

When Max left Lydia's that afternoon, he headed straight to the sheriff's office. He walked in and saw the tall man tacking wanted posters onto the wall and taking down others.

"What can I do for you?" the sheriff asked without turning around.

"I want to talk to you about Horace Belcher."

The sheriff turned slowly and lifted an eyebrow. "I wondered when someone would be around."

"I'm Max Caldwell, from the Walsh Detective Agency. I'm trailing Belcher who's wanted for murder, theft and embezzlement in Chicago."

"That's some accusation." He crinkled his eyes and jutted his chin toward Max. "Who is he supposed to have murdered?"

"Horace Belcher."

"Hoo-wee." The sheriff held out his hand. "I'm Robert McCauley, sheriff in these parts. That's some accusation."

The men shook hands.

"First, do you have any identification?"

"I do." Max pulled his wallet from his jacket. Inside was his badge.

"Good. Now explain to me how Horace is supposed to have killed himself?"

"He didn't, actually. His real name is Gilbert Ross. Until this incident, he was just a two-bit hustler and con artist." Max ran his hand behind his neck and started to pace the office in front of the sheriff's desk. "Then he must have heard Belcher was taking over the bank in Oregon City and would be carrying diamonds. How he learned that closely guarded secret, I don't know. To the best of my knowledge only Belcher and the Walsh Detective Agency knew.

"Anyway, Ross must have decided it was a sweet deal. One he couldn't pass up."

"Oregon's a long way to chase a man," said Sheriff McCauley.

"Ross hit my wife with his carriage as he made his escape. I didn't chase him because of her, though I should have…she didn't die right away and was in great pain."

"Are you after Belcher for the murder of Horace or for the death of your wife?"

"For the murder, theft and embezzlement. Avenging my wife is a bonus."

The sheriff sat behind his desk. "Sit, Mr. Caldwell. We need to talk."

"Don't mind if I do, Sheriff."

"Call me, Robert or Bob. I answer to both. The townspeople haven't decided which to call me yet."

"Okay, Bob. Call me, Max. I have a feeling we'll be getting to know each other very well."

Max explained Belcher's background.

"I'm not surprised," said Robert. "I believe he's been stealing from Walt Mosley for some time but I never could prove it. But more importantly, I also think that somehow he was responsible for Walt's death, but I can't prove that either."

"And now Miss Granger has inherited the money. Do you have any idea how much that is?"

Robert leaned forward on his desk. "According to Walt he had more than half-a-million dollars in the bank. I know he kept a lot of cash at home, but he said having the money in the bank was good for the town, that way there was money to loan the townsfolk."

Max put his foot over his knee and set his hat on the resulting circle. "What makes you think Belcher was stealing from Mr. Mosley?"

"Walt said that every time he'd make a withdrawal, Belcher seemed to get nervous, so much so that sweat rolled down his temple."

"I wouldn't be surprised if he was stealing. He couldn't go straight unless something was about to kill him and even then he'd think about it very hard first."

The sheriff chuckled. "Agreed."

"I have a plan that I think will catch Belcher." Max explained briefly what he hoped Lydia would agree to do.

"Aren't you afraid that action puts the woman in danger, if, Belcher is in fact stealing from her?"

"I plan on protecting her. As much as possible, if need be."

Bob narrowed his eyes. "What do you mean, if need be? This man is supposed to have murdered a man and is inadvertently responsible for your wife's death. How can you think she won't need protection?"

Max put his foot on the floor and leaned forward. "I promise she'll be safe. I'll stake my life on it."

"That's good because if anything happens to her, I'm blaming you and that might include arresting you for her injuries."

Max nodded. "Fair enough." *I failed to protect Anna. I* will not *fail to protect another innocent. I will make sure that Lydia Granger is kept safe.* In the back of his mind was that niggling little doubt. *"What if I fail again?"*

Lydia returned home carrying several packages of meat. As she walked into the kitchen, she heard someone banging around in the pantry and was afraid one of the animals had gotten in there and was making a mess. She set the packages on the counter and opened the door. Relief flooded her when she saw Hannah instead.

"Do you realize how big this pantry is?" asked Hannah.

"No, I haven't done but a cursory glance around the kitchen. Mostly checking the icebox, to see if there was meat rotting in there."

Hannah's eyes widened. "And was there?"

"No, thank God. It was completely empty. I bet the sheriff cleaned out the food. He was Walt's best friend."

Hannah relaxed and pointed at the packages in Lydia's arms. "You better put those down. Did you find a good deal on the meat?

"Yes. I got old cheap meat for the animals. It's not spoiled, but the butcher didn't want to sell it to his regular customers. He was happy to find someone who would buy it for one quarter the regular price. I know I don't need to negotiate such deals any longer, but old habits die hard. Besides just because I can afford to pay full price doesn't mean I should be wasteful."

Hannah clapped once, squeezed her hands together in front of her hips and grinned wide. "A quarter of the price! That's a great deal. How'd you manage that?"

Lydia grinned back and nodded. "It was better than just throwing it away. At least he got something for it, and I told him I'd buy all he has daily."

"Good. Now after you feed your babies. I have a surprise for you. Actually, Mr. Mosley…Walter…left a surprise for you."

Lydia wrinkled her brows. "How could that be? He wasn't even sure I was coming. I did write to tell him we were coming, but he might not have even received it."

Hannah smiled. "I think he was pretty sure."

Unwrapping the meat Lydia separated it onto three plates. She set Trinity on the counter with his, so the other two wouldn't eat his meal. He was at too much of a disadvantage to eat on the floor with the bigger animals.

Picking up Simba while holding a plate of meat for him, Hannah put them both down by the pantry door.

Calling for Sampson, Lydia set his plate by the back door.

After Lydia washed her hands, Hannah led her out of the room. "All right, you've fed the babies. Now come see your surprise."

They shut the animals in the kitchen where their claws could do the least damage and then Hannah led Lydia upstairs to the door next to the master bedroom.

The entire bedroom was done in light pink.

Lydia grinned. "I only told him my favorite color one time. He remembered."

"Oh, the room isn't the surprise. Go to the closet."

Lydia walked that way. "If it's anything like Walter's, it's the size of my old bedroom in Independence."

"Just go inside."

She did and about fell down. The room was full of dresses, skirts, blouses, and shoes. She walked to the chest of drawers and discovered chemises, bloomers, pettislips, corsets—everything she needed for under the clothes.

"But I…I…only gave him my sizes once. He asked in the first letter what I looked like, my dress size and shoe size, my height and so forth. I never thought he'd do this. I just thought he wanted to be able to picture me with him. He must have had them shipped from San Francisco or New York. That's the only way they would have been here before he passed." She closed her eyes for a moment. *Oh, Walter. I do so regret that we didn't meet in person. You were the kindest man I ever knew and still, after you're gone, your kindness remains. Thank you.*

"Try on something. Pick the dress you want to wear for dinner tonight."

Lydia grinned and began looking through the dresses one by one. Twenty-one in all. She picked a dark pink one with long fitted sleeves and a sweetheart neckline that was a little more daring than demure. The dress was a couple of inches too long because he'd had them made to go over the small hoops she saw hanging in the corner. She'd have to ask Hannah to help her take up the hems since she had no desire to wear hoops again.

"Will you help me hem these? You can wear these clothes, too. They'll be just the right length for you."

"Maybe after the baby comes, but for the most part you know I'd rather make my own clothes. These might be long enough, but with me expecting they'll be a bit too snug for me. I might take a couple of the skirts. I can alter those easily enough. With the blouses I already have, those would give me several new outfits, which would be nice."

Lydia waved at the skirts. "Take what you want. But help me put this one on so I can see how I look."

Hannah helped her don the new dress and then buttoned up the back for her.

"Most of our clothes wore out on the trip here on the wagon train. A person can't walk for ten miles every day and not wear out your clothes and shoes. We do have about the same size feet I might see if any of these shoes or boots will fit me."

She realized she was now a very rich woman and being able to make this offer made her feel good. "Take anything you want. You know whatever I have is yours including all that money. You, Joe, and your kids, none of you will ever want for anything.

This money is enough to keep all of us, and our children and grandchildren, very well off. I just wish Walter were here so I could thank him."

Hannah hugged her sister.

"I know, but thank you for giving voice to your generosity, anyway."

A knock sounded at the bedroom door.

"You all decent?" Joe called.

"We're decent. Come in," replied Hannah.

Lydia came out of the closet to check her appearance in the cheval mirror in this room. *Had Walt purchased a mirror for every bedroom?*

Joe stopped as she entered the room. "You look beautiful, Lydia."

"Ah, thanks, Joe. But I just look like me."

"I know, but I never saw you this dressed up. You're almost as pretty as my Hannah."

The aforementioned woman stepped out of the closet. "You're a lucky man since you said 'almost'."

Lydia lifted a brow. "He's a lucky man regardless. He has you and that makes him the luckiest man alive, in my book."

He grinned and took her in his arms. "There never has been and will never be any woman as beautiful to me as you are, my love."

"You do know what to say." Hannah stood on tiptoe and kissed her husband.

"Now if you'll excuse me ladies, I still have more goods to unload from the wagon. They are mostly kitchen stuff, but I don't want to release the animals, so I'm putting everything into the dining room. I just wanted to let you know where I've gone."

"Goodbye, Joe," said Lydia.

"See you soon, love," said Hannah.

Lydia hadn't realized until now how much she envied Hannah and Joe their love. Maybe because she'd been engaged to Walter and was sure she'd eventually have the same thing. Now though, she thought she might be an old maid. She'd never marry now except for love…she didn't need the security anymore. In which case, she might be the old woman in the big house with all the animals or the crazy cat lady on the corner. What else could they come up with to call her?

But then there was Max Caldwell. When she saw him she felt like she'd been pole axed. She'd never been so attracted to a man. She was afraid she'd do anything he asked just to be close to him. Well, almost. If he really wanted her to be bait, he'd have to teach her how to shoot. A derringer was her weapon of choice. She needed something she could keep in a pocket or a reticule.

She ran her hand along the side seam of the dress, the fabric the finest she's ever had and sure enough, there were pockets in the skirt. She reached her hands inside and found them to be quite large. *Plenty big enough for a small gun.* She smiled.

"What are you smiling about?" asked Hannah.

"Just how much I like this dress and how well it fits. Except for the length, it's perfect. Help me out of this. I'll put on my old dress to cook dinner and then change into this pretty new one to entertain Max."

Hannah frowned. "I wish you'd stop calling him, Max. He's still Mr. Caldwell."

Lydia raised her eyebrow and crossed her arms over her chest. "Just like we called Joe, Mr. Stanton?"

Hannah pursed her lips. "That was different."

Lydia's voice rose. "How? How was it different? Because we were on a wagon train? Or because we were out in the prairie somewhere? You're being a hypocrite, Hannah."

Hannah closed her eyes and lowered her chin. "You're right. I'm sorry. I'll just get used to Max, like you did with Joe."

Lydia placed a hand on Hannah's shoulder. "It's all right. You recognize what you're doing and you'll stop. Right?"

Her sister rolled her eyes. "Yes. Of course, I'll stop."

"All right, just two hours and I have a pork roast to prepare along with mashed potatoes, glazed carrots and a cherry cobbler for dessert. It's going to be tight. I picked up some fresh cream for the cobbler."

"Sounds fantastic. Are you sure you don't want more company?"

Lydia laughed when Hannah put on her best puppy eyes face. "You and Joe get leftovers tomorrow…for lunch. Will that do? Then we can have steak or pork chops for dinner tomorrow night. I got both, so you can decide."

"Pork chops. We haven't had those since we left Independence."

Lydia nodded and reached for the buttons on the back of the dress. "That's the reason I chose the pork roast. Now, why don't you go help Joe move our things into the house? We want the wagon emptied so you and Joe can use it to take supplies to your new land."

Hannah helped her with her buttons. "I'm amazed at how many people return back East so quickly. Some of them don't even give it a full year. How can you know if the land will produce if you don't give it time enough to show you what will grow and what won't?"

"They want out of this weather according to Mr. Pearson at the mercantile." Lydia changed dresses and walked out of the bedroom, headed down the stairs with Hannah at her side.

"I can tell you, I won't be returning to Missouri and neither will you. Joe's ranch will be the most successful horse ranch in the area and you both will love it here. I already do, thanks to Walter. He's allowed me to live my dream of having a shelter for lost animals."

When they reached the bottom of the stairs, Hannah hugged her sister. "I'm so glad, Lydie. You deserve some happiness. You took the step to become a mail-order bride and saved us from being on the street."

Lydia put her arm around Hannah's waist. "You would have done the same thing. I just thought of it first."

"I like to think I would have, but I don't know if I would have or not."

When they arrived at the front door, Lydia turned to her sister and gave her a kiss on the cheek. "It's about four o'clock now. I have time to get the meal done if I don't dawdle." She jutted her chin toward the door. "Go on now. Help, Joe. I'll see you later tonight. Come by after you have dinner in town, in time for dessert, say about seven-thirty or eight o'clock. Max is supposed to be here about six-thirty."

Hannah laughed. "Okay. You won't find me turning down dessert."

Six-thirty arrived along with a knock on the door.

Sampson barked and ran down the entry hall.

Lydia opened the door while holding her newest foundling. A baby raccoon she rescued from behind the stove.

Again, Sampson barked and growled at Max.

Max looked down at the animal and his eyes widened, but he held his ground. "Do you know your dog is a wolf?"

She felt a little affronted he would tell her this fact. "Of course. I've had him since he was little. He's only about six months old now and that's actually a guess. Once he gets to know you, he'll greet you with kisses instead of growls, but he is very protective of me."

She heard Simba coming down the stairs. He made what Lydia affectionately called his roar, which was really more of a loud hiss.

Max looked over her shoulder and jerked back his head. "A cougar cub, too?"

"Yes, and an owl in the dining room, which is why we'll eat in the kitchen. I haven't found a good place to put his perch so it's easy to clean up after him."

Trinity wound himself around Max's legs, rubbing up against him. Then Sampson left Max and sat next to Lydia. The little mountain lion ignored the humans completely and instead headed toward the cat, pouncing on it. Then the two began to wrestle on the living room floor.

"Now that you've met my family, do you still want to come inside and talk to me about your plans?"

Max smiled, took off his hat and put it on the coat tree by the door. He handed her the flowers in his hand. He eased his way past Sampson, to stand near her. "Yes, I believe now that the shock is over, I shall do very well with your pets."

She was pleased, feeling warm inside, that he accepted her menagerie. She walked toward the kitchen.

"Come along, Max. They won't hurt you... unless, of course, you attack me."

He shook his head. "I assure you, I have nothing like that in mind."

She grinned. "I didn't think so. Now let's go talk about what you want me to do and what I want in return."

Chapter 4

"Have a seat." Once inside the kitchen, she waved an arm toward the table, set with china for their dinner. "Would you like coffee, tea or water?"

"Coffee, please. Black."

"Very good." She poured him a cup of the dark, rich brew. "Here you go. I take mine with a little milk and sugar." Lydia sat at the table across from him and prepared her coffee.

He took a sip. "That's very good."

"Thanks. We had a lot of practice making coffee on the trip here. So, tell me more about yourself. I think we should get to know each other better before we discuss the scenario you have in mind. I know you work for the Walsh Detective Agency and were a Texas Ranger. Are you married? Do you have children?"

I love children. I hope he has some.

Max nodded, wrapped his hands around his coffee cup and looked down. "I was married. My wife was killed as Belcher escaped. He hit her with his carriage as she was crossing a street."

She reached across the table and squeezed his hand. "I'm so sorry. So you're here for her, too."

"I should be. She didn't die right away and was in great pain while she lived. But my job is to gather the proof to arrest Belcher."

You're fooling yourself, Max. You're here as much or more because of your wife than you are the murder of some random stranger.

Lydia pulled her hand back. "Do you have any children?"

"A daughter. She'll be three tomorrow."

"I'm sorry you're not with her, though I understand why you don't have her along. Is she staying with family?"

"Yes. She's with my late wife Anna's brother, Roy, and his family. It's a good situation for Julia. Their son is just about the same age, so the children have each other to play with."

"What will you do when you've finished with the Belcher business? Return to Chicago?"

"Move back to Chicago?" He pursed his lips. "No. Except for my job, there's not much to keep me there. Anna was from that city, but everyone except her brother and his family have either died or moved away. And Roy is bringing Julia to me and moving his family here. More opportunities, they hope, and a better place to raise their children."

I'm glad he has a daughter and he misses her. He likes children and that is good to know.

"I came as a mail-order bride, as you must know from your research into Walter's background. And into mine, I suppose, if you had the time."

"I knew Walter had a bride coming." He leaned toward her. "I never expected her to be so beautiful."

Lydia felt the heat in her cheeks. "I bet you say that to all the women you want a favor from."

Max blushed to the top of his head.

"No, really. I'm not complimenting you just because I need your help."

Lydia laughed. "I'm teasing. Are you ready to eat? I've been keeping the food warm." She walked to the stove, got the food, placing the roast in front of him.

"Would you carve?" She handed him a carving knife and fork.

"Certainly."

He cut two slices of the roast before glancing over at the animals standing on the other side of the kitchen near the door.

"Don't worry. They won't come until called. They are very well trained, though I like to think of them as polite."

Max lowered his brows and looked much more relaxed.

He served them each a slice of the pork. "How in the world did you train them? A wolf? A mountain lion? But mostly, how did you get that cat to mind you? Cats are notoriously independent."

"I just taught them." She shrugged. "I'd put them back where they needed to stand. I wouldn't feed them until they remained there. After enough times, they got the hint and stayed. I think Trinity did it mostly because the other two did. You're right they were much easier to train than he was."

"Are all your animals male?"

"Yes. An odd coincidence isn't it?"

"The food looks wonderful. I haven't had a real home cooked meal for a long time. Sometimes restaurants come close, but it still isn't the same." He settled his gaze on her. "Of course, enjoyment of the meal could have something to do with the company."

She smiled and dropped her gaze to her lap. "Thank you for saying so."

They finished their meal in relative silence. Lydia smiled as she watched Max glance warily at the animals.

She looked over at her babies. They were lying quietly on the floor and were being so good. She was so proud of them.

"Shall we move to the living room for coffee? Hannah and Joe are coming for dessert."

In the living room, Lydia sat on the same blue wool sofa where they'd had their first conversation.

Max sat in the dark blue brocade arm chair across from her as he'd done that morning. "You basically know the plan. I talked to the sheriff today and he's fairly sure that Belcher had been stealing from Walter."

"Is it possible he killed Walter, hoping to escape with all the money?"

"I don't know, but I doubt it or he would be gone now. I think he intends to go on as he has been. The doctor said it was a heart attack, but the sheriff doesn't believe it. He said Walter was in good health."

Walter's letters never stated anything to the contrary.

Lydia leaned forward. "Heart attacks can disguise lots of cases of murder. I've read certain poisons can mimic a heart attack. Would you or this doctor know if Walter had been smothered? My guess would be—no. But in any case, I want something from you."

He smiled. "Anything. You have only to ask. What do you need?"

"I want you to teach me how to shoot a gun. Specifically, a derringer. I understand Mr. Sharps makes one that would work for my needs."

He lifted his eyebrows. "Interesting that you would ask to learn with that specific weapon. Those guns are not in production yet. I'll have to see if I can have a gun specifically made for you by the local gunsmith. A smaller version of my revolver is the best I can do."

"I assume your statement means you'll also be teaching me how to use it."

Max sat back.

"Yes. I'll teach you to shoot a pistol. You'll practice with my gun until we obtain yours, then you'll practice every day with your own gun until you become used to the weight and feel of it in your pocket as well as in your hand. Even with the weapon being smaller than normal, it will still be fairly heavy and you should probably reinforce your dress pockets."

"Hannah will help me."

"Now to our discussion of my plan. You already understand the gist of it. If my idea works as I want, Belcher will take as much of your money from the bank and run, hopefully to Portland, as that is the closest port. He can probably hide there, or at least will think he can, until the next ship comes in."

"Why do you want him to run? Why can't you just arrest him?"

"Because we never found the weapon and without that we don't have a solid case, just circumstance. I believe he still has the knife with him. Plus, the real Horace Belcher was carrying one-hundred thousand dollars worth of uncut diamonds. Because they are uncut, he won't have been able to sell them yet. He needs to find a jeweler willing to cut the diamonds."

"But why come here and impersonate this man Belcher? Wouldn't it have been easier to just run with the diamonds?"

"Probably, but the real Belcher must have told him about Walter and his money. As you know by now, Walter was a very, very rich man. He used that money to help his community, that's true, but even doing that he was still very rich."

"Yes, I've become aware of that fact. I do want to help you, but I want to learn to shoot first. I think I should introduce myself to Mr. Belcher tomorrow and find out just how much Walter has there, compared to his paperwork here. I found his books in his safe."

Footsteps sounded on the porch followed by a quick knock and the opening of the front door.

Lydia looked up but finished her thought. "Good idea. Hannah can help me with that."

"Help you with what?" Hannah asked as she entered the living room ahead of Joe.

"Help me with Walter's books and reinforce my pockets in my dresses and skirts."

"Why do you need them reinforced?" asked Joe, his eyebrows creased.

"For my pistol, silly."

Joe's eyes narrowed further. "So you talked this man into teaching you how to shoot a pistol. I'm assuming you told him you already know how to fire a rifle."

She cocked her head to one side. "No, actually, proud as I am of that accomplishment, he agreed to my stipulations before I got that far in my negotiations."

Joe took a deep breath and shook his head. "I don't see any good coming from these lessons."

"You're wrong." Max leaned forward and gazed up at Joe. "She needs to know how to protect herself if she's to face Belcher. I haven't told her about his behavior, but I probably should. Otherwise, he might not seem as dangerous as he truly is."

Joe crossed both arms over his chest. "Yes, I think you should. She needs as much information as possible."

"Agreed," said Max.

"Don't forget I'm in the room, gentlemen." Lydia frowned and lifted a brow.

"And me, too." Hannah sat next to Lydia on the sofa. "I'm very interested in this conversation and I expect to be treated with the same respect you do Lydia. In other words, I want to learn how to shoot a pistol, too." She crossed both arms over her chest and stared at her husband.

"See what you've started," grumbled Joe. "And what about the possibility of the gun being taken and used on them?" He sat on the arm of the couch next to Hannah.

Lydia thought Joe was talking to Max, but he might well have been talking to her since she was the one insisting on learning.

"Look," said Lydia. "What you and Hannah decide about her is your business. This situation is my business and I'm learning how to shoot a pistol. You have no say in what I do, Joe."

Max moved to stand by Lydia.

She thought it was a show of support.

He placed a hand on her shoulder. "I won't let her go in the bank without some personal protection. I'll be outside, but it will take me a few seconds to enter and shoot. I want to give her that few seconds. She doesn't have to hit anything. If she shoots him all the better, but her firing will give me the time I need to aim and fire. You're aware of this, Joe. You've been in these kinds of situations before, haven't you?"

"No. I damn well haven't put anyone in danger the way you plan to." He jutted his chin toward Lydia.

"It's not just his decision, Joe. It's mine, too," said Lydia. "I want to get this man behind bars. I don't want him to kill anyone else."

Joe paced behind the chairs, stopped and turned toward Lydia. "This fight is not yours."

"If not mine, then whose? He stole from Walter and now he's stealing from me. Do you really think he's stopped because I'm here now when he wasn't bothered while Walter lived here?" asked Lydia.

Frowning Joe looked over at Hannah. "Why aren't you saying anything? I'd have thought you would be waxing poetic about all the things you could do if you knew how to shoot a pistol."

Hannah tilted her head and narrowed her eyes at her husband. "Because I happen to agree with Lydia. She needs to know. If you plan on leaving me on the ranch alone then yes, I need to know as well. If you'll be around all the time, then I don't need to learn."

Joe sighed. "You're right. There may be times when you're alone and you should know how to protect yourself."

Joe looked over at Max. "Looks like both the ladies will be learning."

"Did you ever think about pretending to be a bank examiner? You could see whether he was actually stealing that way," said Lydia. *Good. I've offered a safer alternative.*

"I don't know enough about accounting to make a believable examiner, much less to know if I actually saw evidence of his stealing. I also don't have the credentials to fool a bank president into opening the banks books, whether there is something to hide or not," replied Max.

"What are you looking for as evidence of his murder of Horace Belcher?" asked Hannah. "I mean that's the whole point of this project isn't it?"

Max stood and ran his hands through his hair. "The diamonds are unaccounted for."

Chapter 5

Max sagged onto the chair. "We never found the diamonds. The real Horace Belcher was murdered while he was in possession of one-hundred thousand dollars in uncut diamonds. I believe that *this* Belcher has those diamonds with him. I need them to prove my case."

"Wouldn't he have sold them by now?" asked Lydia.

"I don't think he's been able to because they are uncut and the only people he could sell them to would be jewelers. He needs to keep a low profile. There is no comparison to the life he lives now compared to the one he lived in Chicago. He lives like a king now. Nice home, money whenever he wants it. Your money, but still he never thought you'd actually show up and Walter was much too trusting. He's even married and has a baby now.

Something he could never have done before," said Max.

"How could he marry that poor woman?" asked Hannah.

Joe put a hand on his wife's shoulder from where he stood behind her. "I doubt very seriously, my dear, that he courted her by revealing he's a murderer. And besides, he's probably providing her and their son with a very good life as the wife and child of the town's only bank president."

Max shook his head, stood and began to pace from the sitting area to the door and back again. "I think she knows who he really is. She traveled from Chicago to marry him and I believe they were in a gang there together. That's another problem he has. He wasn't the leader of the gang and if Seamus Holliman finds out about his new life, there'll be hell to pay. I don't want to see gangs come into Oregon City any more than you do. The sooner I take down Belcher, the sooner the town will be safe."

"Why didn't you tell us that to begin with?" Lydia asked. She began tapping her foot and crossed her arms over her chest. "There is a woman and child involved now. All care must be taken to keep them safe. Regardless, if the wife knew or not, that baby is an innocent. The sins of the father shall not rain down on the child."

Max sat on the coffee table in front of Lydia and placed his hands, palms up, on her knees.

She unfolded her arms and put her hands in his.

He gave them a slight squeeze. "Belcher won't take her and the baby when he leaves. They would slow him down. That's the last thing he wants so they will be safe. She won't even know he's abandoned her."

"Very well, if you're sure, then we'll leave them out of this altogether," said Lydia.

Hannah took Lydia's hand in hers.

Her hand was damp. Lydia saw the worry on her big sister's face.

"Hannah? What vexes you so? If you keep frowning like that, your face will stay that way." Lydia tried teasing her like when they were children.

"Lydia. Stop it. I'm not a child and I'm worried about you. This man talks like…" She waved a hand through the air. "Belcher will just pick up and leave, but what is to stop him from trying to eliminate you? He wouldn't have to leave then. You would just disappear and he'd go on as he is. It's not like he hasn't killed before."

"Or" added Joe, "what if he comes here for the money in the safe and then, kills you anyway once you open it? He's got to know it's here. He was too familiar with Walter. There's too much money for him to walk away without trying to get more of it to take with him. Trust me. I know how a criminal's mind works."

Lydia took a deep breath and nodded. "I know. A lot of variables need to be accounted for before this plan goes into action. But the first one is for Max to teach me how to shoot. To that end we need to see about getting me a small gun."

Joe shook his head and then bent, lifted a pant leg and removed a weapon from his boot. "I keep this Colt here, just in case I need it." The small gun, at least by comparison to his regular pistol, was exactly like his six-shooter. "I had it especially made for me. It takes .22 bullets rather than the .38 that my revolver takes. They may be smaller, but they'll get the job done."

He handed it butt first to Lydia.

She took the weapon and steeled herself for its weight. Holding it barrel down, she was surprised. The gun was not nearly as heavy as she thought it would be.

Joe sat next to his wife. "You can give it to Hannah, when you're done. She'll be able to carry it in her pocket while on the ranch by herself. That shouldn't happen very often, but sometimes I might come to town without her for supplies or something. Who knows what the future will bring."

"I do," said Lydia. "Tomorrow Max will begin my lessons after I return from the bank. Nothing goes forward until I'm confident I can protect myself and my babies, if I need to."

"No," said Max. "Tomorrow, Joe and I will build that enclosure for your animals before they tear up the house. You know how animals are and even though they are very good, they will start marking their territory; their nails will tear up the carpets and the floors just because of the running and playing they do. They need outdoor space for their bathroom needs as well. Soon they'll realize they can jump the fence in front and they'll be gone.

"You're right," said Joe. "I'll get the wire tomorrow morning. We should have the enclosure built by noon."

A few minutes before seven o'clock the next morning, Lydia answered the front door and waved Max inside. "Did you eat breakfast?"

"No. I awoke later than I expected."

"Good. Follow me and join us."

Max raised his eyebrows. "Us?"

"Certainly. My babies and me and Joe and Hannah. They live here, too."

He nodded. "I forgot you consider those animals your family. What happens when you have a real family? Children and a husband?"

"My husband will love my babies as much as I do or he won't be my husband. There is no negotiation on that point."

"I understand. They are a part of you."

"Yes. Exactly."

They entered the kitchen where Joe and Hannah were eating breakfast.

"Sit and I'll make you a plate. Then you and Joe can get to work."

Max sat and Lydia brought two plates to the table, one for him and one for her. His was piled high with bacon, eggs and biscuits. Her plate was not as full.

She got him a cup of coffee. "There's butter and honey on the table. Please begin."

Max buttered his biscuits. "This looks great." He took a bite of the biscuit. "And tastes even better. Thank you."

Lydia felt her face heat at his praise. "Thank you."

After finishing breakfast, Joe went to the general store for the chicken wire and to the lumber yard for the four by fours, for the enclosure. Lydia was surprised to see the wire was eight feet tall.

Joe and Max got started right away.

After about two hours, Lydia brought them coffee.

"You boys need to take a break. Between digging post holes and then nailing the wire to the posts, it will take you at least until lunchtime to make the animal run."

"Once we get the posts in we can finish the enclosure in less than an hour," said Joe.

"And we'll hook it to the house so you can just open the back door and let them out. We'll also make a door so you can go from the pen into the back yard.

"Sounds wonderful. I can't wait to see it."

While the men assembled the animal pen, Lydia dressed in a dark blue serge suit with a pink blouse trimmed down the front and around the bottom of the high collar with white lace. When she was prepared, she set out with purpose for the bank.

Entering the building she walked up to the cashier on duty. "I'd like to see Mr. Belcher." The young man was only a couple inches taller than Lydia and skinny. So much so, his Adam's apple bobbed when he spoke.

"I'm sorry ma'am. Mr. Belcher doesn't see anyone before nine."

"He'll see me. I'm Lydia Granger and if he doesn't see me, I'll close my account right now."

"Oh, yes, Miss Granger. I'll be right back." The clerk hurried away and Belcher came out. He was a balding man, overweight with a stomach so large it entered the room before he did. She covered her mouth to suppress the giggle she felt at that thought.

"Miss Granger. I've been expecting you. I'm so glad you arrived none the worse for wear."

Lydia held out her gloved hand. "Pleased to meet you, Mr. Belcher. I wanted to introduce myself. Now that I've inherited all of Walter Mosley's holdings, I want a full accounting of everything he has with the bank. Deposits, mortgages, loans…everything."

Belcher pulled a handkerchief from his pocket and mopped his forehead. For some reason the man had started to sweat. "Of course, Miss Granger. If you'll give me a couple of days I should have all that information for you."

"Very well. I'll see you in one week's time. That should give us both plenty of time. I want to compare your records with Walters. I should be able to familiarize myself with his books by then. Thank you, Mr. Belcher. Good day."

Lydia turned and left the bank. She knew that Belcher stared after her. She heard him utter "What a bitch" under his breath as she left. She smiled.

After lunch, Lydia jumped up from the table and started clearing the dishes.

Hannah put her hand on Lydia's shoulder. "I'll do this. You and Max go start your lessons."

"Thank you." She kissed her sister's cheek and then turned toward Max. "Come out back. There is no one behind the house so you can teach me there and we can practice without disturbing anyone. I've set up some old cans and bottles I found in the trash barrel. Hopefully they aren't too close."

They walked outside and Max started laughing. "You'd need a rifle to hit them from this distance. Let's move a bit closer, shall we?"

Lydia was a little embarrassed, but Max seemed to take it in stride as they moved toward the targets.

Max pulled Joe's gun from his waist band. "The first thing you're learning is the parts of the gun. You need to know how to take apart the weapon and clean it so that it's always ready if you need it. Let me show you."

Max pulled pins, took out the chamber and, from a leather sack, produced a rod with a piece of cloth through the end, like thread in a needle. He rammed the rod down the barrel several times after putting on a liquid of some kind.

When he was done cleaning the chambers as well, he put it back together and loaded the bullets.

"Now, I want to see if you were watching. I want you to unload and then load the gun."

She took the gun, pointed it toward the ground and did all the same things he had except clean the barrel, before handing it back to him.

"Very good. You really are a quick study."

"I am when I'm learning something very important. This is important to me, not because of the money, but because of the poor murdered man and because of your wife and daughter who I bet is as beautiful as her father is handsome."

Max colored a bit. Then he narrowed his eyes. "Are you flirting with me Miss Granger?"

Her palms sweaty, she hoped her flirtation would be welcome. *What if it's not?* "And if I were, Mr. Caldwell?"

He put the gun in his waistband at his back and stepped close. His hand palmed her jaw and down the edge of her neck to her shoulder. He placed the other hand at her waist and pulled her to him.

"Then I might just have to kiss you. Do you mind?"

"I wish you would and don't bother to ask." She wrapped her arms around his neck, tugged him down to her and mashed her lips against his in a hard kiss.

He stood there and let her kiss him.

She pulled back her head.

He kept his arms around her waist.

"I guess I was mistaken," she said and unwound her arms from him.

He smiled and shook his head. "Not at all, my dear. I simply wanted to see what you know. Have you ever been kissed before?"

"No. That was my first kiss, but I've watched Joe and Hannah. I guess not enough."

"Don't worry about that. Now I'll kiss you like you should be kissed."

He pulled her close and pressed his lips against hers in a gentle kiss before brushing the seam of her lips with his tongue.

She sighed and opened her mouth. They tasted each other, played, dueled, enjoyed.

When she finally pulled back she rested her head on his chest. Exhilarated, her heart pounded in her chest so hard she was sure he could feel it. "Oh, my."

He pushed a strand of hair behind her ear. "Let me take you to dinner, Lydia."

She pulled back and looked up at him. "Do you think that wise? What if Belcher sees us? He might decide there is something between us and scoot before you're prepared for him to. Why don't you come to dinner here, again? We'd have chaperones in Joe and Hannah, but you can always sit on the porch with me or better yet, take me for an evening stroll in the woods behind the house. I noticed a path back there earlier today."

"Belcher may have already seen us. I've been coming to your house fairly regularly, but even so, you're right eating here probably would be the best thing. And given the way I'm feeling right now, chaperones aren't a bad idea either."

"I know." She reached up and ran her hand through his hair. "Kiss me again, Max, and then we should probably get back to the lesson."

He gathered her to him. "I wouldn't miss it for the world."

Then his lips touched hers and the world around her evaporated until there was just the two of them. This man was dangerous, not only to her heart but to the very air around her, and she wouldn't change a thing. Feeling such intense emotions was new to her and she reveled in them.

She fired the weapon five more times, reloaded it and fired it again. She kept that up for about thirty minutes.

Finally, she held the gun pointing down from her limp, worn out arm. "Max, my arm is tired. I can't practice anymore."

"That's fine. You did really well."

"Ha. I barely hit anything until that last round."

"Yes, but you were very tired and still managed to hit half your targets. That is definite progress."

Her shoulders sagged. "I'm glad you think so. I'll see you tonight for dinner.

"Yes, and that walk."

"If I can still manage to lift my arms to put on my cloak."

"I'll put the garment on your shoulders for you."

"Then you have a date, sir." *Despite how tired I feel, I'm looking forward to tonight. Will Max kiss me again?*

Max went directly to the telegraph office from Lydia's. He needed to check in with his office.

The young man behind the counter looked up, smiled and pushed his spectacles up his nose. "Hi, Mr. Caldwell. Wiring your office?"

"Hi Sammy. Yes, it's that time of the week. Have any messages for me?"

"No sir. I remember my instructions. Keep the messages unless it is a matter of life and death and then bring it to you. Otherwise you'll pick them up when you come in."

"That's right. Thank you, Sammy. Just a short message today. Max took the paper and pencil he handed him and wrote the note to his boss, Abner Walsh, son of the founder of the Walsh Detective Agency. *Things going according to plan. LG is cooperating. Max.*

He returned the paper to Sammy. "Get that out when you can. I appreciate it."

Max put a ten dollar gold piece on the counter. Keep the change, Sammy. See you next week."

The young man grinned and picked up the coin. "Gee thanks, Mr. Caldwell. I'll get this sent right away."

"Good. Bye now."

He walked out of the office and headed to his hotel.

Max arrived at the house promptly at six o'clock that evening. He adjusted his bow tie and then knocked on the door, not the least bit surprised to hear Sampson's deep 'woof' on the other side.

Lydia opened the door.

Sampson jumped up, placing his paws on Max's chest.

Max laughed. "Now, boy. Down. Down, Sampson."

Lydia laughed, too. "You have to sound like you mean it. Down. Sampson," she said in a deeper tone.

The wolf put his feet back on the floor and rubbed against Max instead.

"He loves you, Max. I haven't seen him take to anyone as quickly as he's taken to you. Simba and Trinity are the same way."

Lydia was beautiful. She wore a light blue dress the color of the sky when thin ribbons of clouds filled it. Her eyes almost matched, but they were a little darker and the black ring around the outside of the iris was intriguing. He shook his head to get his wayward thoughts back on track.

"How's the baby raccoon?" he asked the ridiculous question to get her a bit off-kilter. She was always so…proper. He'd like to see her rattled occasionally.

"Bandit is doing just fine. He's eating anything and everything I put in front of him. I have to watch him, though. He's very smart and apparently very hungry. I've caught him inside the pantry. I think he's figured out how to open the door, though I'm not sure how since he's so little. Maybe he sneaks in when Hannah or I are in there."

Max smiled. "Bandit, huh? Because of his mask or his sneaking into the pantry?"

Lydia nodded. "Both. The name seemed too perfect to pass up. Come inside. Hannah and Joe are in the kitchen."

Max entered.

She shut the door.

He leaned forward and whispered. "Will they stay there long enough for me to kiss you?"

She nodded. "I've got them both cooking, so kiss me, Max. Kiss me like it's the last time."

He cocked his eyebrow, but did as she asked, putting everything into the kiss. He'd never fallen for a woman so fast, but Lydia was special. Anyone could see she had the biggest heart. All her pets, her devoted sister and brother-in-law, her worry for Mrs. Belcher and the baby.

Lydia was unlike anyone he'd ever met and when this situation was over, he would ask her to marry him. Anna would approve. He'd loved his wife, and he hoped he would eventually love Lydia. For now, he liked her, cared for her, wanted to see her happy and thought he could make that happen.

But what if she said no? What if she demanded his love? Would he walk away rather than hurt her? Could he walk away was the better question. She was getting under his skin and, yes, he felt emotions he hadn't for a long time. But was it love?

What if he couldn't protect her? He hadn't protected Anna and she was dead. He was asking Lydia to risk her life. What if he couldn't protect her either?

Chapter 6

One week later

"We can't wait any longer. I think you've had enough practice," Max said over dinner. "It's time to put the plan into effect."

He came to Lydia's house every day and helped her practice with the gun Joe gave her. Her accuracy was much better, and they'd been working on the surprise factor, as well. After all, she didn't expect Belcher to take out an ad in the paper announcing that he would rob and kill Lydia Granger. Max didn't stay for dinner every night, but tonight he did so they could discuss tomorrow's events. Lydia was as ready as she would ever be.

"Do you really think so?" asked Joe. "I mean I've seen how much better she's gotten, but do you think she's good enough? She's only been training for a week."

"Gentlemen, I'm in the room. Why don't you ask me if I'm ready to put the plan into effect?"

Max covered her hand with his and nodded. "Of course. You have to feel confident enough for this to work. Do you? I know you're worried but we have to do this sooner rather than later. Given Belcher's known propensity to run, I think now's the time, especially since you told him you'd be back."

She had to admit she was both anxious and scared, but Max's belief in her made her feel wonderful and confident. She could make this plan work.

"I'm ready. I'll go tomorrow morning. I've met Belcher now and he knows me. He won't be surprised to see me, but he will definitely be caught unawares when I give him my request."

Max squeezed her hand as it lay on the table. "He'll ask for some time to get that much money together."

She didn't move her hand. The warmth of his over hers, the way contact with him made her feel, she'd leave her hand there all night just so the feeling would never end.

"I'll tell him I just want the available cash in the bank now. After all, I don't want to collect the money that is out for loans to the townspeople. So only the cash on hand and a statement of the rest that the bank owes me. Then I'll ask him to order in the remaining cash from San Francisco. That will take probably a month, won't it? He'll need time to get the letter to the bank in San Francisco and then time for the money to get back here."

Max put down his fork. "There are no large banks in San Francisco and this bank is not affiliated with any bank there, but I don't think he'll believe you know that. Tell him you want one-hundred-thousand dollars. Or fifty thousand. Some number that is sure to make him react, but won't put any of the town in a bind if he decides to give it to you, which I doubt."

Lydia's eyes widened. "I would never do anything to injure any of the people here. They have been very kind."

"You've also helped them by taking their old, sick pets and seeing that they have a good life before they die. The residents appreciate that," said Hannah.

"Lydia, would you care to go for a walk? It's a lovely evening for December in Oregon City," said Max.

"I must do the dishes—"

"I'll do the dishes. You two go on and take a walk," said Hannah.

"I'll help her," said Joe.

Lydia smiled. Her sister was playing matchmaker again and this time, Lydia didn't mind one bit.

"Very well. Let me get my cloak. It is still chilly, regardless that we've been having nice weather."

They walked outside, and when they were out of the yard Max held out his arm for her.

She placed her hand in the crook of his elbow and they walked behind the house, past the animal pen, into the woods. A path, probably an animal trail, headed into the woods. She'd seen it at her daily lessons and wondered where it went.

"Where are we going?" she asked.

"Not far. Just out of sight of the house."

"Why?" She didn't feel any trepidation, not with Max, but she was definitely curious.

Max stopped and turned to face her. "Because I want to kiss you…with your permission, of course."

"You have it. I hope you don't plan on—"

Max's lips covered hers and he pressed them into hers.

Pulse racing and her heart hammering in her chest, she wrapped her arms around his neck as his arms came around her waist and pulled her flush with his hard body.

He touched his tongue to her lips.

She opened and tentatively met him with her tongue.

He pushed into her mouth, tasting her and she him.

Lydia played, pushed, circled, and dueled.

Suddenly he pulled back, but kept his arms around her.

"I want you, Lydia and the feeling scares me. We should head back."

She was feeling wanton and wanted more but giving in to her baser instincts could lead to consequences she wasn't ready to pay.

"You're right. We should go back. Thank you for kissing me." She stepped out of his arms and smoothed a hand down her skirt.

"You never need to thank me for kissing you. It is always my pleasure."

Bothered by his reaction, she wanted to leave and put this episode behind them. "Good. Shall we go?"

Max cleared his throat. "Um. Yes. Let's." He held out his arm to her again and she took it but only because the ground was uneven and she didn't want to fall. As soon as they reached her yard and she could see the path, she released his arm.

He touched her arm. "Lydia."

She jerked away from him. "Don't Max. I wouldn't want to make you *uncomfortable,* so let's just leave it with us being friends."

He replaced his hand and stopped her. "I don't want to be just friends."

She turned to face him, tears welling in her eyes. "Then what do you want, Max? Because I haven't a clue."

He ran a hand behind his neck. "I'm mucking this up." He turned to her and took both her hands in his. "What I want is to court you…properly."

Her eyes widened unable to believe her ears. "You do?"

"Yes. I feel closer to you than I have anyone since my wife died. I'll do my best to be a good husband to you."

Husband? Did he say husband? Heart beginning to pound again, she listened to him. "I hear a *but* coming."

He took a deep breath. "But, I don't know that I'll ever be able to love you as you deserve. I don't know if I have that emotion in me any more for anyone except Julia."

Lydia walked slowly to the porch. When she reached the bottom of the stairs she stopped. "Yes, Max, you can court me. I agreed to a marriage with Walter without love. I suppose I can do that with you as well."

She climbed the four stairs to the porch, then turned and faced him. "I'll see you in the morning." She walked through the front door without looking back, afraid that if she did, her tears would begin to flow.

Why couldn't she find love? Maybe someday, if she was lucky, she and Max would love each other. Maybe.

As he walked back to the hotel at the other end of town, Max shook his head. What was he thinking?

Courting Lydia? Yes, he was more attracted to her than he'd been to anyone in a long time. But he still loved Anna. She'd only been gone a little more than eighteen months. All this time while he chased Belcher, his heartache and vengeance had kept him going, but now? Since meeting Lydia, he felt his heart begin to beat again. For the first time, he thought he and Julia could make a family with someone.

Then again, he wondered if he was just another of Lydia's wounded, abandoned creatures. Placed in an orphanage at the age of two, he'd stayed until he was fourteen, and then ran away, unable to take the brutality any longer. His only regret was that he had to leave behind a little friend. He couldn't take along a small child.

Sean O'Grady would be about twenty-five now. Twenty years was a long time. How had he fared? Had he married? Was he even alive?

Max wondered if he'd ever see his friend again. And if he did, would Sean even remember who Max was? Hearing the tin piano music coming from the saloon as he passed, he thought about going in and drowning his sorrows in a whiskey or two, but that wouldn't help and he'd only feel terrible in the morning.

What brought on these maudlin thoughts? Sean was a man now and had probably forgotten about Max long ago. So why did that five-year-old boy suddenly haunt him?

Max shook his head and cleared it of the troubling thoughts. But he couldn't clear his head of Lydia. She stayed with him every minute of every day. Waking or sleeping she was on his mind.

He changed his mind and entered the saloon. He needed a drink. Maybe he needed to get drunk. Maybe then he could clear his mind of the beautiful blonde woman with the magic touch and gentle soul.

Somehow he didn't think even getting stinking drunk would help, so he decided to have only one. Yes, one would do. Just enough alcohol to relax him a bit. Enough to perhaps let him rest, but somehow, he doubted it.

He wanted…no needed, Lydia in his arms again. Why had he ever let her go?

Lydia checked her reflection in the mirror and patted her hair in place.

"You don't look at all bad." She looked up. "Thank you again, Walter."

She smoothed the skirt of the navy-blue walking suit, tugged down the jacket's sleeves and patted the pocket of her skirt, the pistol quiet in her pocket.

Trinity, Simba and Sampson all vied for attention. She'd already fed everyone. Bandit was asleep in a box behind the stove. The two puppies with the burns hadn't even tried to venture upstairs. They waited for her, tails wagging, at the bottom of the stairs. Tippy, the one with the injured ears, and Tug, the puppy with the burned tail and leg were both leery of the second floor. That's where they'd been when rescued from the fire. They were scared and had a right to be.

"All right, my babies. I'll be back very shortly. I just have to make a murderer unhappy. That task shouldn't be a problem, should it?" She giggled and shook her head. She continued to talk to her animals and people who didn't know her thought she was crazy, but who's to say they were wrong. Maybe it takes a little crazy to do what she was planning. Being bait for a murderer probably wasn't the smartest thing she'd ever done.

Taking a deep breath she walked outside and then headed east toward town and the bank.

Within ten minutes she arrived in front of the Oregon City Bank. Lydia took a deep breath and released it slowly. Then she looked for Max and saw him at the corner of the bank, leaning against the building. She smoothed her skirt, stiffened her spine and walked into the bank.

"Miss Granger." Horace Belcher headed toward her from his office. "What can I do for you on this cloudy day? Thank goodness we are not having rain, too."

She studied his face wondering if his words were genuine. Wondering how much money he'd stolen from her account. "I think for what I want, we should speak in your office."

"Certainly. Come this way." He waved his arm toward the back of the building where his office door stood open, so he could observe everyone who came in.

Lydia went straight into the office.

"Please sit, Miss Granger." He pointed at the leather arm-chairs in front of his desk as he shut the door.

She sat and straightened her skirt as she tried to control her breathing. Being in a room with a thief and murderer was difficult.

"Now," he said as he took a seat. "How can I help you, Miss Granger?"

"I want to withdraw one-hundred thousand dollars."

Horace froze. Then he chuckled. "For a moment I thought you said one-hundred thousand dollars."

"I did."

He frowned. "That sum is a lot of money, Miss Granger? Are you unhappy with the bank for some reason?"

"Not at all. And I don't want to take any of the funds that are loaned out to the townspeople or backing any of the town's projects. I just want the cash on hand over and above those needs."

With his hands clasped on the desktop, he looked coolly at her. "We don't have that kind of money on hand, Miss Granger."

"Then order it from wherever you need to, so that I may have it. The money is mine, Mr. Belcher."

Lydia watched as the man started to sweat. A bead formed at his hairline and ran down the right side of his face to his jaw where it dripped onto his shirt. Either he was totally unaware or if he was aware, he didn't care.

"What, may I ask, do you need so much cash for?"

"I have an investment opportunity I can't pass up."

"Really? What could require that much cash?"

"I'm buying a gold mine in California. I understand that is where Walter made his money. I thought I would try the same thing."

"A…a gol…gold mine! Are you insane?" He stood with his palms planted on his desk. Just as quickly he sat and slapped a hand over his mouth. "Forgive me, Miss Granger. It is none of my business what you do with your money."

She thought he would have apoplexy. Raising a hand to her mouth she hid the smile she couldn't prevent.

Lydia lifted an eyebrow and tried her best to look imperious. "That's right, Mr. Belcher, it is not. The money is mine, bequeathed by my late fiancé, and I'll do with it as I please. If my brother-in-law couldn't talk me out of this venture, what makes you think you can?"

He finally took out his handkerchief and wiped his forehead.

When he looked at the cloth, he seemed surprised that it was damp.

"Well...I...I perhaps you haven't thought this through. Think of what it will do to the town."

Lydia kept her back ramrod straight. "I've already stated I don't want any money from the town or the people. Those monies will stay on loan or on deposit, whatever the townspeople need. If you do anything to hurt these people after I withdraw the money, I will hear of it, and I'll make sure you are removed from your position here at the bank."

Now she saw what she'd been waiting for. Panic and rage. His face was mottled red and white, and he sputtered when he tried to speak.

"You—you—you can't do that. You're just a depositor. You have no say in how this bank is run."

Her stomach turning, she couldn't stop now. Lydia lowered her chin and narrowed her eyes. "I'm the *largest* depositor. Without my money, the bank doesn't stay open isn't that right, Mr. Belcher? I'm sure the bank's board of directors would see it my way. Especially when I tell them that you've been stealing from Walter before doing so from me."

"There is no proof. You can't tell them a lie, you bit—"

She pointed at him with one finger. "Be careful what you call me, Mr. Belcher. I don't take kindly to being compared to a female dog."

Lydia thought he looked like he would explode.

Instead he suddenly calmed. "You do what you have to do, Miss Granger. I can't let you take all of the cash in the bank. Therefore, I'll do my best to have your money in two weeks. It will take that long to send to San Francisco and then get it back here."

So far the plan is working just like they expected. "Very well. I'll be back in two weeks." Lydia stood. "I hope you'll be successful in your endeavor."

Belcher nodded and smiled. "I'm sure I will be. Good day, Miss Granger."

That broad smile worried Lydia. What did the man have planned that he could now smile after nearly having an apoplectic stroke?

She stood for a moment on the boardwalk outside the bank's one-story stone building and donned her black gloves. She saw Max waiting for her still leaning on the building.

As she passed he stepped up beside her. "How did it go?"

CHAPTER 7

"When we get to the house, I'll tell you." She opened the front door and was greeted by her babies. She just kept walking and they moved with her. "Hello, sweeties. Come on, now. Let Max in."

Max followed her, ignoring the animals surrounding him in greeting.

Lydia removed her gloves, put them in her pocket and hung her cloak on the coat tree by the door. She patted Sampson on the head as she walked to the living room sofa.

"Enough. Sampson, go." She pointed in the direction of the kitchen. "Find Hannah."

"I'm here." Hannah stepped into the living room. "I'll put Sampson and the puppies out in the pen in the back yard. They can work off a little of this rambunctiousness."

"Thank you. Being outside will be good for them."

Max leaned forward in his usual arm-chair. "Forgive me for being anxious, but what transpired in Belcher's office today?"

"Well, I—" Lydia calmed enough to finally draw a deep breath.

"Sorry. I'm here now. Joe took the wagon back out to the rest of the wagons. They'll sit there until sold." Hannah grinned and plopped onto the sofa.

She and Joe had been forced to marry, for propriety's sake, but it turned out to be a real love match and they were both very happy to be married. Lydia hoped she'd find such a match and wondered, once again, if the man across from her now was the one she waited for.

Lydia smiled at her sister.

"I'm already tired."

"My wife was tired all the time when she was in your condition, too."

Hannah's eyes narrowed. "I didn't know you were married."

"Max is a widower," said Lydia. She realized she should have shared this detail with Hannah and Joe over the past week that Max had been coming to the house.

"Oh," Hannah's eyes widened and her brows lifted. "I'm so sorry."

Max waved away her words. "It's all right. I'd be protective of Lydia if she were my sister, too."

Lydia cleared her throat. "Mr. Belcher said he needs two weeks to get the money from San Francisco."

"That's bull—"

"Max!" admonished Lydia. "Language."

"Sorry, but as I told you before, this bank isn't affiliated with any bank in San Francisco and there aren't any large banks there anyway. Yours is all the money the bank has. That's all or most of it. Of course, other people have money on deposit, but your money is that which keeps the bank running."

"Then why the story about San Francisco?" asked Hannah.

Max leaned back and crossed an ankle over his knee. "To give him time to get away. If he tells you he has to go to San Francisco to get the money and that it will take two weeks, you won't sound the alarm until after those two weeks have passed."

"He didn't say he would go, but that he would send for it. Perhaps he plans to tell me he has to go himself to escort the money back since it's such a large amount."

Max nodded. "Yes. That would make sense. You would think he's being diligent. When he doesn't return, any trail he might have left would be long gone. But now that we are aware of his plans, I'll keep an eye on him and follow him when he bolts."

"Should I be worried?" Lydia crushed her skirt in her hands. It didn't matter what Max said, she was already worried. She'd seen Belcher's face before he'd suddenly changed. He was a desperate man.

"Well," Max ran a hand behind his neck.

The gesture was one he made when he was frustrated.

His agitation did nothing to calm Lydia's nerves.

"I think you need to be very aware of your surroundings. I believe your animals will protect you as much as they can, when you're here, but they are still young. Just remain on guard, as will I."

"Joe and I will, too. We'll postpone our trip to the land?" said Hannah as she reached over and squeezed Lydia's hand.

"Don't be silly. I have my gun and Max will be following Belcher. I'll be fine. You and Joe need to get your ranch started."

"Well, I think that's all that can be done for now." Max stood. "I better get back and start watching Belcher."

Lydia stood, too. "I'll walk you out."

Hannah grinned and then hid it behind a hand.

Lydia looked down at her sister and frowned.

Hannah sat up straight and stopped smiling.

If Max wondered what was happening between the sisters he didn't mention it. Though once they got to the door and out of Hannah's sight, he did smile and wink at Lydia.

"If you were alone, I'd kiss you."

His statement left her feeling warm inside. "And I'd let you."

"This gesture will have to do for now." He brought her hand to his lips and placed a chaste kiss there. "Be sure and let me know if you notice anything out of the ordinary."

"I will. Thank you."

"No, thank you. I wouldn't have a chance to recover those diamonds and prove his guilt without your help. You're amazing."

Lydia felt the telltale heat in her cheeks and knew she blushed.

He released her hand and ran his knuckle down her cheek. "You're so beautiful. Inside and out."

No one had ever talked to her this way and she admitted she liked the words. Liked hearing that he liked her. "You don't have to flatter me. I'm already helping you."

"My darling, I'm not flattering you, simply stating a fact."

Warmth radiated from the center of her being. "Thank you. As much as I don't want to, I must let you go. I have to care for my animals."

He opened the door and walked outside away from the house.

She watched him until he was out of sight, then closed the door and leaned her back against it.

"That was a long goodbye," said Hannah. "You like him, don't you, Lydie?"

Lydia nodded and wrapped her arms around her waist. "Yes. I do. Quite a lot, but he says he can't love me and I don't think I'll get as lucky as you and Joe. He loved you from the beginning though he didn't know it and fought against it."

Hannah put an arm over her sister's shoulder. "Men never think they can fall in love. They believe it to be a *problem* that only affects females. Rather than a wonderful feeling that makes life even more beautiful."

Lydia smiled. "Said like a woman in love."

Hannah nodded. "And I am. I love him more than I ever believed possible."

Joe walked in from the kitchen and walked directly to Hannah. "I'm glad to hear it." He took Hannah in his arms and kissed her as though Lydia wasn't even there.

"Uh hum." Lydia cleared her throat. "That's enough, you two. Don't make me any more jealous than I already am."

"Sorry." Joe held Hannah close with both arms around her waist. "I just want to take advantage of anytime we aren't in public and have to watch what we say and do. We already push the boundaries of what would be considered proper back east."

"Then it's a good thing we aren't back east," said Hannah, with her arms around Joe's waist.

"Yes, it is." Joe kissed her on the tip of her nose and released her. "Now I put the last of the things from the wagon, mostly kitchen stuff, on the counters."

"That's fine. It's funny, but I'm looking forward to cooking with my own, old pots and pans and using our plates to eat from."

"I know. Isn't that strange? I was thinking the same thing and yet Walter probably bought you all this new kitchen stuff. I feel almost guilty for not wanting to use it."

"Maybe I'll donate the items to the church. They can give it to some poor people who need it, unless you know of anyone specific?"

"What about Dorothy McInroy?" Hannah turned away from Joe. "She lost everything when the Huckabee wagon went over the cliff. It was only by chance she wasn't in the wagon, too, but she didn't like the way Esther and Ruth were driving the animals. They were racing mules and the sisters acted like the wagon was in a race. So sad."

"You're right. I'll get in touch with Dorothy." Lydia shook her head and sighed. "It's too bad none of the clothes Walter had made for me will fit her, but she's almost six feet tall."

"That's the truth. She's only about two inches shorter than I am," said Joe.

"If the dresses will fit her elsewhere, I can add a flounce to the bottom to make the dresses and skirts longer. Or I could use the material I have for you and make her dresses instead."

Lydia hugged her sister. "You're a good woman and good friend. I'm sure Dorothy will appreciate whichever the answer turns out to be."

"I saw Dorothy going into the mercantile when I came past." said Joe. "You can probably catch her there."

"Good. Let's go."

"You go," said Hannah. "I'll stay here and help Joe pack things onto the buckboard he bought."

"I'm taking Hannah to see the land we bought. I've got the first of many loads of lumber to take there," said Joe. "I want to spend a few days, looking it over, and start building the barn. We can live in it while we build the house and the rest of the out buildings. We'll see you again on Saturday, that's just four days. I'm sure you'll be fine without us. Max will be here most of the time anyway, won't he?"

Lydia shook her head and laughed. "Probably. For now, you just want to get me out of the house so you can be alone. Fine. I'll go. Just make sure you don't let the babies in the room with you. You'll scar them for life."

Hannah waved her away. "Go on, find Dorothy. We'll see you Saturday around noon. The land is only ten miles away or two or two and one half hours by wagon. You know how slow wagons can go. Luckily this one won't be as loaded down as the one we traveled here on."

"All right," said Lydia. "I'm going." She grabbed her cloak from the coat tree and set out toward town.

There was a knock at the door.

Lydia answered. Max greeted her with a grin.

"Oh, you're just in time to escort me on an errand."

Max frowned. "You shouldn't be going out on your own. You just threatened Belcher. There is no telling what he might do before he gets the money and runs."

"Then it's a good thing you showed up."

Max put out an arm and Lydia put her hand through the crook in his elbow. They were passing the alley between the bank and the block with the mercantile when someone knocked Max out with a club and then grabbed her from behind, covering her mouth and hauling her into the alley.

"Don't scream Miss Granger. I don't want to have to shoot you. I just need you to get me to the coast. I know that he," Belcher jutted his chin toward Max's still body. "Followed me from Chicago, but with you along, he won't dare come close."

Lydia knew if she let Belcher take her, she'd never see the light of day again. He would kill her as soon as look at her. She jabbed her elbow into his midsection and when he released her in pain, she ran screaming out toward the boardwalk.

She felt the pain in her side before she heard the gun shot. She heard footsteps running from her, and then a horse galloping away.

Lydia pressed her hand to her side and managed to get up. "Help me, please." Her voice was nearly gone and she couldn't scream for the pain wrenching through her side. She reached the boardwalk and then the corner of the mercantile, before her legs gave out and she slid down the wall of the building to her knees.

People pressed in around her, but she didn't know how long she stayed there before she felt strong arms picking her up.

"Miss Granger, I'm taking you to the doctor and then I'll come back for Max Caldwell. He's awake but not walking just yet and I can't take you both at once."

Lydia nodded and rested her head against Robert McCauley's chest.

The next thing she was aware of was the doctor talking.

"Miss Granger. I have to remove the bullet. From the brightness of the blood I don't think the bullet hit any organs, but I won't know for sure until I get it out."

Lydia nodded. "Do what you have to, Doctor."

"I'm putting a cloth with a few drops of ether over your mouth and nose. The medicine should help with the pain."

What if I don't wake up? What about my babies? And Max? How's Max?

The doctor laid the cloth over her face and used an eyedropper to apply the clear liquid to the material.

That action was the last thing Lydia knew until she woke up in a bed.

"Ah, the lady awakes," said Max. He stood and went to her. "I'll get the doctor. He wouldn't let me take you home until he knew you were no longer under the effects of the ether, which was fine by me." He took her hand. "How do you feel?"

"So how do you know I'm not under the effects of the ether?" She opened and closed her eyes, trying to decide if she was really awake and why she felt so...dull. "I'm not sure how I feel. My side hurts."

"It should. You were shot and the bullet removed from your right side. It should hurt, though the ether is probably still giving you some relief."

She noticed Max had a bandage around his head. "I remember now. Someone hit you with a club and then he grabbed me. Belcher?! How is your head?"

"I'm fine. Head wounds just bleed a lot so the doctor wrapped me up."

The room she was in was small. The table she lay upon dominated the room. A chest of drawers graced one corner and the chair in which Max had sat in the other. Warm blankets covered her and for which she was thankful. The more awake she became the chillier she got.

"You're awake and talking to me so the ether is wearing off." He reached over and squeezed her hand. "I'll be right back. Let me get the doctor."

A couple of minutes later, Max returned with a man in his thirties or early forties with brown hair and kind blue eyes. Her eyes were closed in pain earlier so she didn't see him.

"Miss Granger, I'm Doctor Wade. Glad to see you awake. I think you'll be right as rain in a couple of weeks. The bullet came out of your side clean and didn't hit any organs or anything else vital. You're young and should heal nicely, though there will be a scar that will no doubt be ugly. I apologize for that."

"I don't care what the incision looks like, as long as I won't die. Although, right now I feel like I'm dying of thirst and I have a dull pain in my side. Will it get worse?"

The doctor chuckled. "I'll see about getting you some water but you definitely won't die. As to your pain, it might get worse, but it also might get better. Now I've loaned Mr. Caldwell my buggy and he will take you home then bring the buggy back. Do you have someone to look after you?"

She gazed down at her hands. "Yes, my sister and brother-in-law live with me."

"Good. You'll be bed-ridden for a while and will need them to see to your food and anything else that you need."

"They will. I'll be fine."

She didn't dare tell him that they wouldn't be back for four days. If she did the doctor wouldn't let her go home, and she couldn't stay away from her babies that long. They needed to be taken care of. The animals had already missed one meal if the night outside the window was any indication.

"I'll be back to get you as soon as I bring the buggy out front." Max turned toward the doctor. "What do I owe you, Doc?"

"Two dollars will cover it."

Max pulled out his wallet and handed the doctor a five dollar bill. "Keep the change doc, you deserve it. That's for being here when we needed you."

"That's my job, Max. To help."

Max left to get the buggy.

After he was gone, the doctor looked at Lydia and sat on the bed beside her. "Are you sure you have someone to care for you?"

"Yes, sir. I'll be okay. Really."

"All right. I've given Max some laudanum to give to your sister. You can take up to five drops every four hours. I don't want to give you any more because the stuff can be very addictive."

"I'm not in pain now and I'll only take the medicine if I need to."

He patted her hand. "That's because you haven't moved yet. When Max carries you out, your body will come awake and you'll be glad I gave you the bottle. As a matter-of-fact you should take some now before you start your journey home."

"If you say so. You're the doctor. I'll do whatever you say. I want to get better as soon as possible.

She should tell him she'd be alone tonight, but her animals needed her. They depended on her for their very survival. They came first. They needed her, even if no one else did.

Chapter 8

Max carried her to the buggy and gently set her on the front seat before getting in beside her.

The pain hit her full force as soon as he moved her. The laudanum wasn't working yet and she couldn't help but to cry out.

"Are you all right? I know you're not comfortable, but the trip will be short."

She took a deep breath and let it out slowly. "I'm fine. Let's just get me home. You must have other things you need to do, like find Horace Belcher."

"Sheriff McCauley has deputies out looking for him now. I'm not needed yet. I will see you home and pass along the doctor's instructions to Hannah and Joe."

Her stomach tied itself in knots.

No. I can't let you come in. Then you'll know I'm alone. I have to be able to care for my animals.

"You can just tell me, I'll tell them."

Max narrowed his eyes and cocked his head. "Is there something you're not telling me?"

"No. Nothing." She denied it almost too quickly and wondered if she'd given herself away, but she didn't think so.

They arrived at her home and Max set the brake before coming around to gather her in his arms.

"The gate will be a little tricky to open with you in my arms."

I need to walk my body is beginning to ache all over, like someone beat me up.

"You don't have to carry me. I can walk."

"I like carrying you. I like the feel of you in my arms."

Lydia loved hearing his words. He made her feel special…almost loved. "Then lean down a bit and I'll unlock the gate. It will latch itself again after you close it."

"Okay."

Once they were on the porch, she handed him the key.

He narrowed his eyes. "Aren't Hannah and Joe here?"

"Well, they might be outside and not hear us."

He set her on her feet, for just a moment, while he opened the door.

Returning the key he then picked her up again and carried her through. *This is such a romantic gesture, like a groom for his bride. Will I have that someday? With Max? Not if I keep lying to him.*

The animals all surrounded him, but none of them jumped on him like they normally did.

"That's odd."

"What's that?" she asked through gritted teeth. Being set down and then picked back up jolted her and her injury pained her something terrible. She wished the laudanum would start working.

"Usually your babies are all over you and me, but they are staying back."

"Maybe they sense I'm injured and I'm tired."

He thought a moment. "Yes, I suppose that could be it. Quite unusual."

"Would you take me to the kitchen please? I have to see to their suppers."

"Won't Hannah and Joe do that? I should take you right up to bed."

Her stomach was tied in knots as she admitted her subterfuge. She looked down. "I sort of fibbed when I said someone was here to take care of me."

"Sort of fibbed?" His voice lowered "Just how much *fibbing* did you do?"

Her lips turned down as she pursed them, waiting for his explosion when she told him the truth. "Joe and Hannah will be back on Saturday about noon. I'll be fine until then."

"Fine!? That's four days from now!"

Max closed his eyes and his lips moved like he was counting to ten.

"You'll probably bleed to death from trying to do things you shouldn't."

He carried her to the kitchen and eased her into a chair.

"I've watched you feed them all enough I know what to do."

"But I will do it."

"You won't. I'll do it."

"You won't be here, after tonight."

"Yes, I will. I'm not going anywhere tonight or any time until Hannah and Joe return."

Her eyes widened and her voice rose. "You can't stay here. What will people think?"

He fed the animals and while he was at the counter cutting up the meat, he turned to her, pointing at her with the knife in his hand. "I don't care what they think. I'm not leaving you to fend for yourself after being shot. You're braver than any woman I've ever known, but you're also the most stubborn, contrary female I've come across in all my thirty-four years. You're not getting your way this time. I'm staying."

"Fine. Do you think you might help me to my room?"

He shook his head and sighed. "Yes, as soon as I've finished with your babies."

After he washed his hands, he scooped her into his arms and carried her upstairs without even getting winded. *Max is so strong.* She loved and needed his strength now, and though she didn't want to admit it, she was very glad he was staying.

At the top of the stairs he stopped.

"Which room is yours?"

"The first one on the right."

He carried her into her room and set her on her feet beside the bed.

"I need to get out of these clothes and into a nightgown. Then I'll go to bed."

"Where is your nightgown?"

"Third drawer of the chest of drawers in the closet." She pointed.

Max walked into the small room whistled. He returned a minute later carrying her favorite white nightgown.

"What will you do with Walter's clothes?"

"I don't know. Give them away I suppose. Can you wear them?"

"Perhaps. I didn't know Walter to make the comparison. He died a week before I came to town."

"Oh. Right."

"Can you get undressed by yourself?"

"Yes, I believe so."

"Then I'll go downstairs and rummage around to find something to fix you for dinner."

"I'm not hungry. I'm very thirsty though. There's water in the pitcher on the table." She jutted her chin toward a table and two chairs in front of the window nearest the bed.

"Let me get you a glass, and you can start undressing. I'll stay if you think you need help."

"I'll let you know after I unbutton this bodice."

I can't let him see me undressed. That would be the most improper event in this whole improper situation. Oh, God, what have I gotten us into?

She reached for the top button and found her hands weren't as nimble as usual.

An after effect of the ether, perhaps?

Or maybe she was just too tired or too weak to undress herself.

Lydia sat on the bed, unable to deal with any more and let the tears fall.

She looked up when Max returned carrying a glass of water. When he saw her crying, he hurriedly put the glass on the nightstand, sat next to her and put an arm around her shoulders, before gently pulling her to him.

She tried to embrace him but the movement pulled on her stitches in her side.

"Oww. Getting shot isn't fair."

"No. Your getting shot definitely isn't fair. I'm so sorry, Lydia."

"I volunteered. I thought the experience would be fun, a little excitement and yes, a little danger. Perhaps, if I hadn't tried to run, if I—"

Max gently placed his fingers on her lips. "This result is not your fault. None of this is your fault. It's mine for asking you, for not figuring out another way, but mostly the fault lies with Belcher.

He's the murderer and I should have realized he'd do anything to get away. Now, will you let me help you into your nightgown?"

She nodded and sniffled. "It's either that or I sleep in these bloody clothes until Hannah returns. I'm sure you'll be a gentleman."

He smiled. "I'll do my best."

Max rose and helped her to stand. He quickly undressed her. Even though she was embarrassed to her toes, her stomach wiggling as she shed more clothing, she was pleased that he kept his gaze averted as much as possible. Finally, she was in her nightgown and bloomers. She untied the tapes at her waist and let the bloomers fall to the floor, where she stepped out of them.

Max turned down the covers on the bed.

The little bit of exertion she'd put forth to undress sapped her strength, and she sagged onto the bed.

"I'm tired, Max."

He fluffed the pillows, putting both of them behind her. "Lay back." Bringing up the blankets to her chin, he tucked her in.

"I need to rest." She smiled. "For some reason, I'm not feeling very well."

"Okay. I'll go now. If you need anything call me."

"I will. For now, I think I just need to sleep."

"I agree. I'll check on you in an hour or so." He leaned down and kissed her on the forehead. "Sleep."

"Yes, sir. That's a command I definitely want to comply with."

Max walked out shutting the door behind him.

Noon, the day after the shooting

"Max." Her voice was barely a croak. What was the matter with her? She was so hot. Lydia threw back the covers, trying to cool her overheated body.

Lydia sat up then stood, her legs so wobbly she wasn't sure they would support her. She tried to take off her nightgown but it hurt to raise her arm, so she pulled the arm from the uninjured side out and pulled the nightgown over her head then slid the garment off the arm on the injured side all the while keeping that arm straight to her side. Then she walked to both windows, used her good arm to open them wide. A cooling breeze wafted through the room.

"What are you doing? You can't stand naked in front of the windows, someone will see you."

"I'm too hot to care."

Max put an arm around her waist. "Come with me back to bed. I'll cool you down."

"No. You make me hot, Max."

He looked at her and creased his eyebrows. "Look me in the eyes, Lydia."

She did swaying against him.

"All right now, just lie down and I'll be right back. I'm just getting several washcloths, extra bandages and a basin full of water."

He came back, put all the items on the nightstand and then wrung out the washrag in the cool water. Then he wiped the cool cloth over her face and neck.

"Does that feel better, sweet?"

She nodded. "Mmm. Better."

"Good. That's very good."

"I want you to do this forever. I don't know why I'm so hot."

"You aren't well, my dear. I'll cool you though."

"Will I die, Max?"

"No, you won't die. I will not allow it."

She relaxed under his ministrations.

"Lydia. I need to change your bandage. Your wound is seeping blood. It's not anything to be concerned about, just a normal part of healing, but you need to sit up. On the plus side, you'll feel the breeze more and stay cooler."

"Help me sit up, please."

Noting the weakness in her voice, he took her arm and pulled her to a sitting position.

"That's a good girl. Now let's see what we have here."

Max removed the bandage and saw that one of the doctor's stitches was loose. He knew enough from his days as a Texas Ranger, to know he couldn't redo the stitch, but also that she wasn't in danger at this point.

The loose stitch was letting the wound seep, but he didn't think it was enough to be a problem to her healing. He took an extra washcloth, folded it in quarters and pressed the fabric against the wound.

"Let me know if I'm hurting you."

"How would I know? Everything hurts."

His shoulders slumped.

If I could take her pain I would in a heartbeat.

"Sweetheart, I'm so sorry. When the deputies find Belcher, and I've no doubt they will, they'll send me word. Then I'll meet them and give him a bit of payback for you."

What's the matter with me? Why do I want revenge now instead of justice? Because he hurt Lydia.

She grabbed his arm with her good one. "Don't leave me, Max. Please, don't leave me, no matter what."

How can I think of leaving her? Even when Joe and Hannah return, I won't be able to turn my back on her, will I? Even to get Belcher?

"Hush, now. I won't leave you alone. I'll wait until Hannah and Joe return before I do anything about Belcher."

"Good, but not right now."

He smiled. "No. Not right now."

Pressing several cloths against the wound, he applied as much pressure as he dared without hurting her.

"Put your hand here for just a minute." He had her hold the material in place while he wrapped the bandage around her small ribcage. "There. All done. You can lie back and I'll continue wiping you down."

"No, I don't need to be cooler anymore. I'd like to get under the covers now."

"Okay, we can do that." He covered her and tucked her in. "Better?"

"Yes. Thank you. I want to sleep now."

"Sure. I'm just downstairs. Are you getting hungry at all? Should I prepare food for you?"

"I'm not hungry. Just thirsty." She closed her eyes. "Oh, Max, I hurt so much."

"I know." He pushed her blonde hair, normally so beautiful, but now lank from sweating, off of her forehead. "I wish I could take away your pain. Let me fix you a dose of laudanum. It will help you feel better and sleep, too."

"Okay."

Max put five drops of the drug into half a glass of water.

"Here you go. Drink it all down."

She drank it quickly.

"More, please."

He poured her another half glass of the cool liquid hoping that would be enough to quench her thirst. She didn't look good. Her skin was flushed and her breathing shallow.

She drank the second glass of water almost as quickly as the first, but she didn't ask for another. She suddenly groaned in pain. Tears formed in her beautiful blue eyes. She closed them and grimaced but didn't cry out.

"It's all right, you can cry. I don't mind."

Lydia turned her gaze on him. "Do you really think I'm not crying because of you? Whether I cry or not is up to me and has nothing to do with you." She took several breaths and couldn't seem to catch hers.

Max was taken aback, but he supposed she deserved to be angry. He was the one who'd convinced her to do the act, assured her it wasn't very dangerous. He was wrong. Very wrong. He'd underestimated Belcher, but he wouldn't make that mistake again. No, when he saw Belcher next time, he'd arrest him and ask questions later, unless, of course, he was already in the sheriff's custody.

"Call me when you need me."

"I will."

She closed her eyes and turned onto her left side.

He let her rest. That was what she needed now more than anything.

Lydia slept for the next two days except to take her medicine and sip a little of the beef broth he'd made. She needed the broth a lot more than her pets did the bones.

He dozed off and on for those three days in the pink bedroom next to hers, afraid to go farther than the kitchen in case she woke up and needed him.

Max sat reading in the living room when Sampson came in.

He barked then howled.

Max threw the book on the sofa and ran up the stairs to Lydia's room.

He heard her before he saw her. Her teeth were actually chattering. She shivered under the covers. Max hurried to the pink bedroom and grabbed all the blankets from the bed. After carrying them back, he laid them, doubled, over Lydia, tucking them tightly around her, trapping whatever warmth her body put off.

Her shivering didn't subside. He lay down on her good side and added the weight of his limbs to her covers, hoping some of the heat from his body would work its way through.

She calmed, sleeping again.

Glad the situation had been averted, he relaxed next to her,.

Her bed was very comfortable and he was exhausted from being up for the last twenty-four hours. He fell asleep.

Max was awakened by the bed shaking.

Lydia shivered uncontrollably again.

He made the only decision he thought he could.

Chapter 9

Worry crawling through his gut, Max quickly undressed, and then he uncovered Lydia and undressed her so they were both naked and her body could accept all of his heat. He laid her back on the bed and crawled in next to her, covering them both with the blankets. Then he spooned her, his chest against her back, his legs over hers and his arms wrapped around her. He touched as much of her skin with his as he possibly could, willing her to absorb his heat.

Her shivers finally slowed, though they didn't completely subside. But she slept, and finally, so did he.

"What in the hell?" shouted Hannah.

Hannah never cussed. What was the matter with her? Lydia was so warm and comfortable. She hadn't slept so well since leaving Missouri.

Lydia moved and was met with a warm body. A warm, naked body. *What the hell?*

Her eyes shot open.

"Lydia, it's me. Max. Do you remember anything?"

Remember? Yes, she remembered everything. Remembered being so cold until Max climbed in bed with her and gave her his heat. She owed Max her life. If he hadn't stayed with her, the fever or the chills would probably have meant her death.

"Yes, Max. I remember. Thank you for saving me."

"You're welcome. Anytime, sweet girl."

Joe came into the room and started laughing.

Hannah put her hands on her hips and tapped her toe. "What's so funny?"

"Lydia has to get married now just like we did." He looked over at Max then narrowed his gaze. "Don't even think of trying to get out of this. You're marrying my sister-in-law, Max Caldwell and nothing more to say."

"I know," said Max.

He sounded resolved. Lydia wasn't sure that's how she wanted her husband. No, she knew that wasn't how she wanted him.

"Max did nothing wrong. He saved my life."

Hannah's eyes widened and a single word issued from her. "What?"

"Belcher shot me and Max was keeping me from dying from the chills. He bathed me when I had a fever; he took care of the babies and me. I'm not forcing him to marry me after all he's done."

Max tightened his hold on her. "No one is forcing me to do anything. But you and I are getting married. No wife of mine will have her reputation in shreds because of a decision I made."

Hannah shook her head and waved her hands in front of her. "What do you mean you got shot? What in heaven's name has happened while we've been gone?"

"Now that I'm feeling better, let us get dressed and then we'll come downstairs and talk. You might start breakfast, I'm suddenly starved and the animals haven't been fed yet either."

"The butcher dropped by more meat for the animals. He was concerned when Lydia hadn't come in on her regular day." said Max.

He hadn't released her, refused to let her out of his hold. She had to admit she kind of liked being held so close.

"I see," said Hannah. "So the butcher knows you are here?"

Max nodded. "He knows and he knows Lydia was shot. I assume the whole town knows by now. I've been finding pies, casseroles, fresh bread and other baked goods by the front door. The town is showing their admiration for Lydia and her kindness."

Lydia was touched that the town would show their appreciation when she was laid up, but didn't want to concentrate on their gifts. "I want pancakes for breakfast."

"All right. Pancakes. We'll go downstairs and I'll make you breakfast, while you two become presentable," said Hannah.

"The sooner you leave the sooner we'll be dressed," said Lydia.

"I'm leaving." Hannah turned on her heels and stalked out of the room.

"Do you want to dress first?" asked Max.

"I'd like to but I don't think I can do it alone."

"Okay. Eyes are closed."

Lydia scooted to the edge of the mattress, stood and nearly fell back onto the bed. She was a little light-headed either because of the injury or from being in bed for four days.

Once she was standing, she put her hand over the bullet wound and walked into the closet. She'd moved her clothes here.

For today, she chose a white blouse and black wool skirt with a jacket that matched the skirt. Her hair was dirty and limp and she stunk from sweating with fever and lying in bed for four days. Lydia knew a bath would make her feel better, but she didn't know what the doctor thought about getting her wound wet. For now she would make a spit bath work and remember to ask Max if the doctor had given any instructions about bathing.

She'd moved a vanity under the window in the huge closet, a good-sized room itself. Finding her brush, she started with the ends and worked her way up until all the tangles were gone.

Before walking back into the bedroom, Lydia called out. "Are you decent?"

"I'm dressed, you can come in."

She walked into the bedroom where Max waited. He'd combed his hair, and though he hadn't shaved in four days she liked his scruffy look. As a matter of fact he looked good enough to eat. *Where did that thought come from?*

Lydia took a deep breath, smoothed her hands over her skirt and straightened her back.

"I'm ready."

"You look beautiful."

She ducked her chin a bit. "Thank you. Walter had good taste in clothing, both men's and women's."

Max walked over and lifted her chin with a single finger. "I'm glad you didn't know him. I wouldn't be marrying you if you'd married Walter, now would I?"

His lips covered hers and he held her there with nothing but a single finger and the press of his mouth on hers.

She enjoyed the kiss and let it go on for much longer than she should have before pulling away.

"Max. I don't want to marry you…not under these circumstances."

He frowned. "So you do want to marry me?"

She sighed and cocked her head. "Didn't I just say I don't want to marry you?"

He placed his hands behind him. "You said under these circumstances. I don't like them either, but they are what they are. We *are* getting married."

Shaking her head, she walked out of the room and headed down to the kitchen, holding her side.

Max walked beside her.

"I won't marry you."

"Sure you will."

She took a couple of breaths and blew them out. "Even if I said yes, it would still be a couple of weeks. After breakfast, I'm headed back to bed and out of these clothes."

Max stopped and took her arm, forcing her to stop, too.

"Are you in pain?"

"Yes. It's much more painful to walk around in these clothes than I thought it would be."

He didn't say a word, just grumbled and scooped her into his arms.

"Max!" She buried her face in his shirt as the pain rolled through her.

"Bed or kitchen?"

She shook her head, the pain in wrapping her arms around his neck was too much to even try.

"As long as I'm up and already in pain, let's go to the kitchen. I'm hungry."

"Your wish is my command."

"Except about getting married."

He nodded and walked down the stairs. "Yes. Except that."

She sighed. Max was the most stubborn man she'd ever known. Too bad she was in love with him.

Lydia laid her head on Max's shoulder.

She wanted to cuss and flail and throw a tantrum, but those actions wouldn't change things and it wouldn't make Max fall in love with her. He told her he still loved his dead wife. Lydia couldn't blame him for that. She was probably a fantastic woman and had taken care of their little girl and Max. Never needing or wanting an adventure, like Lydia apparently did. Why else would she have agreed to this venture in the first place?

"Very well, Max. We'll get married when I'm well."

"Nope. Today."

She lifted her head and stared at him. "Today!? I understand that for propriety's sake we must wed, but does it really have to be today?"

He nodded. "Yes, because I'm not leaving. I don't care that Hannah and Joe are back. I'm responsible for your safety and I want to be with you night and day to provide that safety."

She gave her head a shake. "You don't have to do this."

"I disagree. My reputation is as much at stake as yours. I don't want to be known as some sort of cad."

"I never considered your reputation in all of this. I'm sorry." She was suddenly nauseous. "I never wanted us to get caught in bed or you to have to stay or to save my life. I just wanted to be able to care for my animals."

"I didn't want to marry you this way, either. That is not why I got into bed with you. I want to make that perfectly clear. But regardless of what we wanted, the situation has happened and we'll deal with the situation responsibly"

"Yes, of course."

They arrived outside the kitchen.

"Please, let me down. I don't want to scare Hannah and Joe into thinking I'm worse off than I am."

He stopped and set her gently on the floor.

She smoothed her skirt, took as deep a breath as she could, pasted a smile on her face and walked through the door into the kitchen. Hannah and Joe sat at the table, each with a cup of coffee in front of them.

Hannah stood as they entered the room. "How are you feeling? You look a little pale."

"I'm feeling much better." Lydia sat at one end of the table, as was her right as head of the house.

"You must be starving. I haven't fed you more than beef broth since the shooting," said Max.

"Thanks. I am." Lydia closed her eyes for a moment and then smiled, anticipating the taste of hotcake, melted butter and warm maple syrup.

"Everything is ready. I've got a plate in the warming oven just for you, so you could start when you got here." Hannah walked to the stove.

Lydia smiled. "That's very kind of you, sis. I'm glad you're back."

Hannah turned toward Lydia. "Anything for you, you know that. And we're glad to be back. I felt like we were on the wagon train there. Sleeping in the wagon, cooking over a fire."

"When are you headed back to your property?" asked Max.

"Want to get rid of us already?" Joe cocked his eyebrow and grinned.

"No. I simply want to make sure you are here for the wedding."

"Wedding!" squealed Hannah. "You agreed to get married? I know what it's like to be forced into a wedding, but getting married could be the best thing to happen to both of you. It was for Joe and me." She stood next to Joe with her hand draped over his shoulder.

He put an arm around her waist. "I couldn't agree more."

Lydia tried to look happy, she really did. But to her horror, she burst into tears.

Max was there immediately, kneeling by her chair. "What's the matter, Sweetheart? Don't cry. I promise I'll be a good husband."

Lydia shook her head. "I know you will be. I don't know why I'm crying."

"Well, I do," said Hannah. "You've been shot, had fever then chills, and haven't eaten much so you're weak. Now you find out you have to marry a virtual stranger." She glanced at Max and shrugged. "No offense. If you don't marry, doors won't be closed to you because of your money, but they will be to Max. And polite society will always be talking behind your back about," Hannah made quotation marks with her fingers. *"What you did."*

"No offense taken," said Max.

Hannah moved next to Lydia and put an arm around Lydia's shoulders and squeezed her close, then kissed her forehead. "If you want to slow down and make sure you're well enough to do this, then that's exactly what we'll do."

Lydia shook her head and clasped Max's hand. "No one is forcing me. I'm just worried about my babies. What if they don't like your daughter, or she doesn't like them? I'm well aware that she is more important, but then I'd have to find good homes for all of them. Doing so will be almost impossible for Sampson and Simba. And—" she sniffled and blew her nose on the kerchief Max offered.

"Shh, now. No one is getting rid of your animals. We'll teach Julia how to act around them so they will love her as much as they do you."

She reached over and touched his whiskered jaw. "You're a good man, Max Caldwell. I think you'll make a fine husband. I don't want either of us to acquire poor reputations in our new town. That's not a good way to start. We'll get married as soon as Reverend Trowbridge can perform the ceremony."

Max took a deep breath. "If you're sure, then I'll talk to the good reverend after breakfast and find out if it's possible we could be married today. I'm of the opinion the sooner the better."

Lydia took a couple of bites of her breakfast before pushing away the plate.

"Lydie? Are you all right?" Hannah reached for her sister's hand.

"I don't feel well." Lydia closed her eyes and fell sideways.

CHAPTER 10

"Lydie!" Hannah held tight to Lydia's hand so she didn't fall out of the chair.

Max lifted Lydia into his arms. "Will one of you go for the doctor while I take her upstairs?" *She did too much too soon. I should have insisted she stay in bed.*

"I will." Joe grabbed his hat off one of the pegs by the door and raced to the front of the house.

"Hannah, follow me. I can undress her, but I'm sure she'd much rather you did."

"Of course."

Max took the stairs two at a time. When he reached the bedroom, he set Lydia on the edge of the bed.

Hannah removed her jacket.

"Oh, my God," said Hannah. "Her blouse is soaked with blood."

Max's heart started to pound. "I knew it was too soon for her to be out of bed."

"Max, hold her while I remove her blouse."

He held her by the waist until Hannah had the garment off, then he held her by her shoulders.

"Washcloths, towels and bandages are on the table." He nodded his head toward the window with the table under it. "Get them, and the basin with water. We'll wrap her again."

"Should we wait until the doctor gets here?"

"We'll try and stop the bleeding. Hand me a couple of those washcloths, please."

Hannah gave him the cloths.

Max pressed several of them against the wound, applying as much pressure as he could in an attempt to stop or at least slow the bleeding.

Lydia hadn't regained consciousness and that fact worried him.

He soaked through the cloths and got more, but he cleaned the injury before again applying pressure. The single loose stitch was now three. She would have to be sewn again. Hopefully, the doctor would make the stitches smaller and tighter this time so they stayed closed.

About twenty minutes after he'd left, Joe returned with Doc Wade in tow.

Frowning, Doc went straight to the bed and examined Lydia.

"I need to stitch the wound closed again, after which I want her to stay in bed for at least a week.

Ten days would be better. This injury is not a splinter in her finger that she can forget and go about her work like nothing happened. Her wound is major, and if she doesn't follow my instructions, she's liable to bleed to death."

Max felt a stab to his chest. The doctor's prediction scared the hell out of him. "I'll make sure she stays in bed this time. I shouldn't have let her get up today. She's had fever and chills but looked so much better today I thought she would be all right if she got up for a short while. I was wrong."

"Yes, you were. But now that action doesn't matter. Let me clean her up after I wash my hands and then I'll restitch the wound."

Doctor Wade scrubbed in the basin with Lydia's lavender soap. Then he wiped the wound with the same soap, rinsing and drying the injury. He gave Lydia a small amount of ether so he could stitch and then bind her tightly.

"Leave her in that binding for the next three days. She'll probably be uncomfortable and want to get out of it. Don't let her, and most certainly, don't you do it for her." He shook a warning finger at Max.

"I—" said Max.

"*We*—won't let her talk us into it," She stood by the door both arms around her waist with Joe next to her an arm over her shoulder.

Max held Lydia's hand. "How long before she wakes up, Doc?"

"Probably a couple of hours. She lost quite a bit of blood and it will take that long for the ether to wear off. If she needs help easing the pain, you can still give her laudanum every four hours. Six drops this time in a little water, every four hours. You can give her up to twelve drops at one time but use as little as possible, as the medicine is addictive."

"Okay, Doc. Thanks. How much do I owe you for the house call?" asked Max.

"Nothing. I should have stitched her better."

Hannah showed the doctor out.

Max pulled up a chair to the bed and sat holding Lydia's hand.

"Will you stay there all day?" asked Hannah when she returned.

"Only until she awakens. Then I'll go talk to the reverend. I'll ask him if he can come by tomorrow and marry us." He looked at Hannah. "She needs me, though she won't admit it."

Hannah lifted an eyebrow. "Do you love her?"

Max looked back at Lydia. "I feel as much for her as I'm capable."

"Hmpft." Hannah slowly shook her head. "I've heard that before. I hope it's enough. My sister is the kindest, gentlest, and most soft-hearted person I know. She deserves to be loved."

Max gazed at Lydia and then back at Hannah. "I don't deny all those things. All I can do is my best."

"Did I hear her say you have a daughter? Julia?"

As he thought of Julia, Max smiled. Her golden brown hair naturally curled in to ringlets and her big blue eyes were full of laughter, just like her mother's. She ran to him every night when he came through the door.

"Yes, she's three. I'm looking forward to seeing her."

Hannah placed a hand on her stomach bump. "You must miss her a lot, especially since losing your wife."

"I do. The hardest thing I've ever had to do was to bury my wife and then travel almost immediately to chase after Belcher, leaving Julia behind. She didn't understand why Daddy was going away."

"No, she wouldn't have. She's too young. Are you afraid she won't know you when she sees you again?"

Max nodded and looked at Lydia resting in the bed. "To be honest, that situation terrifies me."

Hannah jutted her chin toward her sleeping sister. "Will Julia accept Lydie and her animals?"

"I think she'll love them. At first, she'll be excited about Lydia's babies. When Lydia teaches her how to treat the animals and they come to like her, she'll grow to love Lydia, too."

She frowned. "Which is more than you can say…at the moment."

Max took a deep breath as regret clamped his gut.

His throat tightened. "I refuse to lie to Lydia and say something that I can't feel, though I care for her greatly."

"Well, I can't fault you for not lying to her. I think you should talk to Reverend Trowbridge now. I want to see you and Lydie married as soon as possible." Hannah looked away from Lydia and over at Max. "For some reason, she said yes to you. You and I both know she doesn't have to marry you, regardless of what people think. They won't treat her as a pariah because of her money, but she said yes to your proposal. She must care for you."

Max stared at Lydia and felt a flicker of hope. Did she care for him? Was it possible she loved him even though she knew he couldn't feel the same way?

Hannah draped the light blue jacket over Lydia's high-collared nightgown which would work as a blouse. "I don't see why I can't get dressed and come to the living room for the ceremony."

"Don't you remember the last time you got out of bed?" Hannah put her hands on her hips. "Well, we do, and we're not going through that again. You didn't hear the doctor's statement that if you didn't rest, you could bleed to death. Well, we did and you'll stay in bed like the doctor told us you should."

"He didn't tell me."

Smiling Hannah crossed her arms over her chest. "Only you could make a nightgown look like a wedding outfit. You look beautiful, even though you're a little paler than normal."

A knock sounded at the bedroom door.

Max peeked in. "Are you ladies ready for us?"

"We are," called Hannah.

Max entered, followed by Joe and Reverend Trowbridge.

The reverend walked to Lydia and took her hand. "I'm so sorry, child, that you are injured and unable to enjoy your wedding day. Don't you Granger girls know how to get married without a shotgun, so to speak?"

"Circumstances have prevented us celebrating our wedding, but it's quite all right, Reverend. We'll celebrate when I'm well again."

"Of course. Of course. Shall we get on with this?" He turned and looked at Max. "Mr. Caldwell, if you will come and stand by the bed we'll get started. I'll need your middle names, please."

"Sebastian," said Max.

"Jeannette," said Lydia.

"Very good. Thank you." The reverend made a quick note on a small piece of paper.

Max walked over and clasped Lydia's hand. "You ready, sweet."

She gazed up at him. "I'm as ready as I'll ever be."

The reverend opened his Bible to a bookmarked passage.

"Dearly beloved. We are gathered here in the presence of these witnesses and in the sight of God, to wed these two people. If anyone knows of a reason why these two should not be married, speak now or forever hold your peace."

He looked at Hannah and Joe, neither of whom said or did anything.

"Very well. Do you Maximilian Sebastian Caldwell take this woman Lydia Jeannette Granger to be your lawfully wedded wife? To have and to hold, in sickness and in health, for richer or for poorer and to keep thyself only unto her, for as long as you both shall live?"

"I do." Max's voice was loud and clear.

"Do you have a ring?"

"Yes." Max pulled a plain gold band from his vest pocket. Then he took Lydia's hand in his.

"Good, repeat after me. With this ring."

"With this ring."

"I thee wed," said the reverend.

"I thee wed," repeated Max. Then he placed the ring on Lydia's finger.

She was glad she'd taken the huge diamond ring off. It had taken greasing her finger with lard to do it, but she'd done it the day after she put it on. It got in the way of taking care of her babies.

"Very good." The reverend looked at Lydia. "Now, do you Lydia Jeannette Granger take this man Maximilian Sebastian Caldwell, to be your husband? Do you promise to love, honor and obey him, in sickness and in health and to keep yourself only unto him for as long as you both shall live?"

She might have trouble with the obey part of the ceremony. The thought made her smile.

"I do."

"Do you have a ring?"

"No, I don't." She wished she'd thought to have Hannah go and buy a ring, but she just wasn't thinking straight. She had too many other things on her mind.

"I have one," said Max. "I bought matching rings."

He handed the band to Lydia, who eased the ring onto the third finger of his left hand.

"Now that rings have been offered and accepted, then by the power vested in me by the Lord, God Almighty, I pronounce you man and wife. You may kiss the bride."

"Gladly." Max leaned down and gave her a very sweet kiss.

Hannah, Joe, and the reverend all clapped.

Sampson barked which caused the puppies to yip.

Simba and Trinity hissed and meowed from the foot of the bed.

"Congratulations, Mr. and Mrs. Caldwell," said the reverend.

"What do I owe you, Reverend?" asked Max.

"One dollar, please."

Max reached into his wallet and then gave the reverend a dollar bill. "Thank you, kind sir."

The reverend smiled. "Thank you."

"Hannah hugged Lydia. "I'm so happy for you."

Then she hugged Max. "Welcome to the family."

Joe gave Lydia a kiss on the cheek and shook hands with Max. "Glad to have another man in the family."

"Reverend, would you like some coffee and dessert?" asked Hannah. "I baked a pie this morning and made a fresh pot of coffee before the ceremony."

The man tucked the Bible under his arm. "That would be lovely. Thank you."

Hannah hooked her hand through the crook in the reverend's arm and walked out of the bedroom.

Joe followed, calling the animals.

Max and Lydia were suddenly alone.

He sat next to her on the bed.

"What do you want to happen now? Are you hungry? I'll bring you a tray. Or are you tired? Here, let me help you out of that jacket."

"Thank you, I'd appreciate that. Not having to move my arm does help with the pain."

Max plucked the jacket from her shoulders.

"I'll hang up this garment and then you can tell me what you want to do."

He left, returned a moment later, and sat on the bed facing her. Picking up her hand, he examined the ring on her finger.

"I'm sorry it isn't fancier—"

"I love it. I love that you bought matching rings. The gesture was very thoughtful."

"I'm glad you like them."

I like that you're holding my hand. I like your touch. It gives me goose bumps every time.

"The ring is perfect for me. I don't have to worry about losing a precious stone while I care for my babies or for having my ring scratch them when I hold them. This band is the only kind I would wear. Thank you." She squeezed his hand and then pulled hers back crossing her arms over her stomach. "Now I think I'd like some of that pie Hannah told the reverend about and maybe a glass of milk instead of coffee."

Max stood. "I'll be right back."

Lydia watched Max leave and then threw off the blankets. She got out of bed and went behind the screen in the corner of the room where the chamber pot was kept.

Half way back to the bed, the room began to spin. She closed her eyes hoping to stop the motion, but when she opened them nothing had changed.

Suddenly, her knees buckled, and she fell to all fours on the floor.

"Max!"

Chapter 11

"Here is m'lady's wedding dessert."

He saw Lydia on the floor with her eyes closed. His heart skipped a beat and fear assailed him.

She lifted her head. "Max."

He set the tray on the tall boy by the door and went to Lydia. "Here now. We can't have you on the floor." Max picked her up and laid her on the bed. "Are you injured?"

She shook her head. "Nothing but my pride. I can't even relieve myself alone."

Max sat next to her and smoothed a wayward lock of hair behind her ear. "You're weak from being in bed. The doctor said you can't take the risk of opening your stitches again or I'd have you walk around the room to build back up your stamina. But he said complete bed rest for a week."

"I understand. In the meantime I want to hire someone to help me with the animals, even after I'm well."

"That's a great idea, though finding someone to work with wild animals might be difficult."

"We'll start interviewing as soon as we begin to get responses to the ad you'll place in the newspaper."

Max pulled a notepad and pencil out of his pocket.

Lydia cocked her head and lifted a brow. "You keep paper and pencil in your pocket?"

"As a Walsh Detective agent, it's become habit to always be prepared to take a statement. Now tell me what you're looking for."

Lydia lifted her hand and ticked off her requirements for an assistant.

"They must love animals of all kinds. They must be willing to learn. They must be willing to live here…with room and board included. Salary to be negotiated."

Hannah appeared at the door. "Excuse me, but there's a man at the door to see Max."

His eyes widened and he pointed at his chest. "Me?"

Hannah smiled, crossed one arm over her waist and rested the elbow of the other on top while she covered her smile. "Actually, he asked if Maxie was here."

"Maxie?"

Could it be? No, surely not. Not after all these years.

He turned to Lydia. "I'll be right back."

He hurried down the stairs and saw a tall, young man holding his hat and standing just inside the door.

Max approached. "Can I help you?"

The man turned, a huge grin on his face. "Maxie."

Max stared. The man had brown hair, a mustache and was about Max's height. He wore a blue chambray shirt, black wool pants, and a holster with a Colt revolver. But his deep blue eyes and smile were unmistakable. A smile that haunted Max's dreams for years after he'd left the orphanage. "Sean? Sean O'Grady, is that you?"

The man nodded. "I go by John now. John Grant. I run into less ignorance that way."

Max knew exactly what he was talking about. Those of Irish descent were considered to be less than decent people and mostly were out-and-out hated. The bigotry, the idiocy, was rampant all through the states.

"Come in. Let me take your hat."

John grinned, handed Max his hat and then stopped moving, except for his widening eyes.

"John? What's the matter?"

The young man backed up a step and pointed. "Th...that's a wolf."

Max turned and saw Sampson sitting about ten feet behind them.

Why hadn't he barked? Because I'm here, maybe?

He smiled. "Yes, he is. His name is Sampson and he's my wife's pet."

John looked at Max and lifted a brow. "Her pet?"

"Yes, she—"

Simba ran out of the kitchen, Trinity on his heels. Suddenly, Simba stopped and Trinity jumped on his back. Both little cats bumped into Sampson, who barked and joined the melee.

"My wife has some unusual pets."

"I'll say. But when did you get married? I hadn't heard and the people who said I'd find you here called this the Mosley place."

"That's all a long story, but as far as marriage…" Max held up his hand where his new ring sparkled. "Just got married this morning. Come upstairs and meet my wife, then I'll get you something to eat and some coffee."

As they climbed the stairs, Max asked. "So are you staying in the area or just passing through?"

"I think I'll stay. The opportunities here are as good as anywhere I've been."

They stopped outside the bedroom door.

"My wife, Lydia, was shot a few days ago and the doctor has put her on complete bed rest, otherwise I'd bring her to the kitchen."

John looked at Max. "Shot? Are you sure she's up to visitors?"

"She'll be delighted to meet you. To meet someone I consider my little brother."

Max knocked on the door and peeked around it. "Lydia, I have someone I want you to meet if you're up to it."

Lydia turned her gaze to him. "I'd love to, but I need that jacket that I wore this morning before I meet anyone."

"I'll get it."

Max returned with the light blue jacket and again draped it over her shoulders.

"There. Ready?"

She nodded. "Bring in your friend."

Max went to the door. "Come in. She's ready."

John walked over to Lydia and extended his hand. "I'm pleased to meet you, Mrs. Caldwell."

She accepted his hand and shook it. "Oh, that sounds so strange. Please call me Lydia." She turned her gaze to Max. "No offense meant."

Max shook his head. "None taken. I know using and hearing Mrs. Caldwell will take some getting used to."

The young man returned his arm to his side. "And you please call me John. I understand you just got married."

Lydia nodded. "John, why don't you tell us about yourself?"

"Not too much to tell. After my parents died last year, I decided to find Max. Luckily for me he didn't leave Chicago. I remembered him saying he wanted to be a policeman when he grew up. We used to play cops and robbers. He was always the cop." John laughed.

Max turned a nice pink shade and chuckled.

"Anyway I checked all the police stations in Chicago and then one of the desk sergeants told me about the Walsh Agency. One day I was reading the paper and saw Anna's obituary." He gazed at Max. "I was sorry to hear about your wife, but the obituary sent me to your brother-in-law, who told me where to find you. I went to Independence, got hired by the first wagon train I could find that was coming this way and here I am."

Lydia put her fork across the top of her plate. "Well, I'm glad you're here. We have an extra bedroom and you can stay with us for as long as you like."

"Yes," said Max. "Please stay. We can catch up."

"I'd hate to be a bother," said John with a wave of his hand.

Lydia shook her head. "No bother at all."

"There, see, you'll stay," said Max, smiling wide. "Now I think we should let Lydia rest. The doctor wants her to heal and rest is the best thing for it."

"It has been very nice to meet you. When I can get out of this bed, we'll visit more."

"I'd like that." He looked over at Max. "I'll wait out in the hall."

"Thank you. I'll be there in a minute or two."

John waved him off. "Take your time."

Max kissed her on the forehead. "I'll leave you to rest now. You should try to nap. The more you can sleep the better."

"I definitely wanted to meet John. He seems like a nice young man."

"He's older than you and Hannah. Not young compared to you."

She shook her head and pursed her lips. "You know what I mean."

Max chuckled. "Yes, I know you were being polite. And you're right. I'd say he got lucky and had good parents."

"You'll have to talk to him about finding work. Can he help you? Perhaps you could open a detective agency here."

"Oregon City isn't large enough for a detective agency but I'll think of something. After this business with Belcher is settled, I need to find work to do myself."

"Maybe you could take over the bank. It needs a new president and I have some pull with the bank's owner."

First his eyebrows furrowed and then his eyes opened wide. "Owner. You own the bank?"

She nodded against his chest. "I found the paperwork in Walter's safe. He started the bank to help the city grow. I believe that Walter was the one who hired the real Horace Belcher."

"Belcher had to have known that fact."

"Yes. Perhaps that's why he thought kidnapping me would help him, though I'm not sure I understand why…unless he knows about the safe."

"You can bet he knows about that. He and Walter were apparently on good terms until Walter found out about the stealing. Belcher won't leave all that money. Not when he can have it and the diamonds, too. Do you want to keep your jacket or shall I hang it again?"

"Thank you. Please put it in the closet."

He took the jacket and hung it up. When he returned Lydia sat straighter in bed.

"Max we need to talk about us."

"I know. The wedding happened so fast your mind must be a whirl of emotions right now. Mine certainly is."

"Yes, it is. But I want to talk about our…marital relations." Heat traveled to pinpoints in her cheeks, but embarrassing or not she had to discuss the situation. "I know you will let me heal before *demanding* your rights, but I'd like more time even after that. I like you a lot, but I don't know you well enough to give myself to you. I'm not ready."

Max sat on the edge of the bed, facing her. "Why don't we see how you feel after you've healed and you've gotten used to sleeping with me?"

Her eyebrows shot up. "Sleeping with you?"

"Yes. I intend to sleep with you, in this bed, from now on. Since I'll be here anyway, I don't want to continue to sleep in the pink room. Besides, how would that look to John if I'm in another room? We're not aristocracy. In America, husbands and wives sleep together."

"Well…I…didn't think about John, so I suppose you're correct." She took a deep breath and let it out slowly. "To that end, you should move your belongings from the hotel and while you're at it, you should see if you can wear Walter's clothes. Or perhaps John can."

"I'll do that later today while you're napping. Are you all right? Did meeting John and this talk with me take too much out of you?"

"No. I'm fine. Tired, but that is to be expected. I do think I'll take that nap now though."

"Of course. I'll get my clothes and be back before you awake."

"Will you eat with me tonight? I'm tired of eating alone."

He picked up her hand and kissed it. "Of course, my sweet. I should have thought of that before now. I'll return later this evening with dinner."

She nodded and watched him walk out, but her mind whirled with thoughts about their marriage. A niggling thought stayed at the back of her mind and she couldn't seem to get rid of it.

What if Max only wants me for my money? He's already said he won't love me. So why marry me?

He's been attentive.

I can't complain about that, but can I really live in a loveless marriage? One where we are just friends? Can he ever get over Anna's death and realize that I'm alive and I need him to feel more for me than "caring"?

Chapter 12

Lydia awoke to a dark room. "How long have I slept?" she said to herself.

"About twelve hours."

Lydia shrieked.

"Shh. Lydia. It's me. Max."

She calmed, though her heart still raced and she panted trying to catch her breath. "Max?! What are you doing in my bed?"

"We got married today, remember?"

As all the memories flooded her, she quieted. "Yes." She took a deep breath and released it. "Now I remember. Your friend John is here, and so you have to sleep with me."

Max chuckled and propped himself on one elbow. "That reason is part of it. The other part is you're my wife and I belong in the bed with you."

"Why? Walter arranged separate rooms for each of us, though there is a connecting door through the closet. The arrangement made it much easier to move my clothes into this closet and move some of Walter's into the pink bedroom closet."

"I can see how that would have aided with moving the clothes, but it doesn't help in the begetting of children. You do want children don't you, Lydia?"

"Yes, very much. Also, I'd rather no one was given the pink bedroom next door. I like having the privacy the room provides…the buffer from the rest of the bedrooms."

"As you wish."

"I'd also like to hire a woman to help around the house and with the animals. Joe and Hannah won't always be here to help and I'd like someone to help clean, feed the animals, cook sometimes and whatever else comes up. They must be flexible."

"We already discussed this. Perhaps I should ask the doctor if loss of memory is due to the laudanum."

"No, you won't. You'll be working. President of the bank, remember? Now who's having memory problems?"

"You're pretty sure I'll take the position, aren't you?"

"Of course. Who better to keep track of our money and help the city grow?"

"Our money? I didn't marry you for your money."

"I know, but now that we are married you know as well as I do my assets now belong to you and I'm hoping you'll share yours with me."

"I don't have much in the way of assets."

"You have one very important asset. Julia. I'm hoping you'll help us to become friends."

"I will. Almost nothing would make me happier."

"Almost?"

"Yes, I'd like us to be more than friends but that situation will come."

"I'm sure you are right. Eventually."

After ten full days in bed, Lydia sat on the familiar table in the doctor's office.

"This will be easier if you lie down," he said to her.

Thrilled to finally be getting the stitches out, she had already removed her blouse and laid down on her left side, so he could work on her right side. He worked quickly to remove the sutures.

"You can sit up and put your blouse back on."

She stood, her back to him and dressed when she was covered she turned back to face him.

Doc Wade creased his brows. "Now, Lydia. You can go back to your regular activities, but don't push yourself. If you get tired, then lie down. You will have to build your stamina back up and pushing yourself to exhaustion is not the way to do that, unless you want to end up back on bed rest."

She shook her head vigorously. "Oh, heavens, no. Just the thought gives me chills. If I get tired I will definitely slow down. And we've just hired a young woman to help me. Her name is Henrietta Cooper, but she likes to be called Hetty."

"That's wonderful. I'm pleased to hear it, but surprised you found someone who is comfortable with all your wild animals."

"She came in on the wagon train and was already aware of my animals. She'd even visited a couple of times. She declined to marry the man waiting. He'd lied to her. Told her he was young and rich, while really he was old and poor. Just wanted a wife to look after his seven kids."

Doc shook his head. "Seven hellions, if you ask me. The only widower I know with seven youngsters is Josiah Kettle. And they need to be arrested not mothered. They are long past the point where having a mother will help. Even the youngest, Ethan, who is only three, is beyond redemption."

She finished tucking in her blouse. "Yes, that's the man, though I doubt very seriously the three year old is as bad as you say. He's too young."

The doctor shrugged. "You believe what you wish, but you don't know that family. Your young lady did well to turn him down."

"Well, we have a bedroom off the kitchen for live-in help and she fits the bill beautifully."

"I'm glad you're getting some help." Doc Wade sat at the desk and chewed his lip. "Um, I need to ask you, since you have such unusual animals as pets, do you take other animals as well?"

Now that she was dressed, she sat in one of the two chairs he had next to the desk. "Of course. I never turn away an animal in need. If we don't protect them, then who will?"

"I'm glad to hear that. I know someone whose dog is about to give birth to the second litter of puppies in a year. The owner doesn't want them and says he'll drown them. I thought if you could take the mother and puppies when they come…"

Her hands formed fists. "Drowning puppies! That's barbaric. Yes, of course, I'll take them. You can either have him bring the little family to me or I'll send someone for them."

"I'll have him drop her off…she hasn't had the puppies yet. He's not really a bad person. He simply can't care for more than one dog."

She shrugged. "Unfortunately that's the case many times, but that is no excuse for killing a helpless animal."

"Thank you, I'll tell him. You are looking great and healing well. In another week or so, I expect you to be right as rain and back to doing everything you did before being shot."

Lydia stood and held out her hand. "Thank you, doctor. Max will be glad to hear I've gotten a clean bill of health, as will my sister and brother-in-law."

She went out to the waiting room where Max sat reading and shared the good news.

Max kissed her cheek. "That's wonderful."

He shook the doctor's hand. "What do I owe you?"

"Nothing. This is still part of the same service."

"Thanks, Doc. You'll understand if I say I hope not to see you too soon."

The doctor laughed and nodded. "I agree. I don't want to see either of you except on a social visit."

Max held the door for her as they left the doctor's office.

"It's so cold now. Was it this way when we got here?"

"No, the weather has definitely cooled. We must have a storm coming in."

"I'm very glad to have my cloak with me. Have you decided whether or not you're taking the job as bank president?"

"I've been thinking about nothing else," he grinned. "Almost, nothing else anyway." He held out his arm. "Shall we go home?"

He helped her into Walter's buggy. She still had a difficult time thinking of everything as hers.

"Aren't you glad we brought the buggy? The weather is much too cold to be walking."

"I agree." After she was settled on the seat, she placed her hands in a beaver muff to keep warm. "I'm also glad Walter saw fit to include coats with all those clothes he had made for me."

Max whispered under his breath. "Walter didn't miss a trick."

She looked over at him. "What is the matter with you? Walter is gone and you're my husband. You are even wearing his clothes, most of which don't appear to have been worn. The perfect wardrobe for a bank manager. Have you decided yet whether you're taking the job? If you're not, then I need to advertise for someone."

He snapped the reins on the horse's rumps. "I'm taking the job and I'll be asking John if he wants to be my vice president."

She smiled and leaned against his shoulder. "Good. That is what I was hoping you'd do."

"Why is it so important for me to take this job?"

"Because I don't want anyone saying you married me for my money. If you have a job then the arrangement looks better for us."

He slapped the reins on the horse's rear ends again. "You care a lot what other people think. Why?"

She quieted her voice almost to a whisper and she looked down at the muff in her lap. "We were treated differently when everyone thought my father was having an affair with my aunt. Even though it wasn't true, we were all treated like pariahs."

"I'm sorry."

She shrugged. "My father was able to ignore it, but the rumors nearly broke my aunt. She attempted suicide and would have succeeded if my mother hadn't found her in time. Aunt Faith eventually did die, but not because of suicide."

His brows creased. "How can you be sure?"

Her gut twisted a little more with every word, but she wanted him to understand her and why she did certain things. "My mother watched her like a hawk does her babies. She kept the laudanum under lock and key and went through my aunt's reticule every night. She searched her room daily when my aunt was out. She did the best she could to prevent it and I believe she succeeded."

"Sounds like she had everything well in hand."

She looked down at her lap. "I think she did, and I don't want any scandal to touch me or Hannah. I don't know if Hannah still wants to open a dress shop. It would be difficult with them living so far out of town, but I suppose if she wants it enough, she'll figure a way."

"Maybe they'll decide to live in town and have the horse property managed by someone they trust."

She sighed. "Perhaps. I'd like that."

They reached home and Max pulled the team to a stop, set the brake and came around to help Lydia out of the buggy.

"Max. There appear to be people waiting on the porch. Were you expecting some one?"

He looked over at the house and saw half a dozen people…and animals. "I think they are here to see you. Look they all have animals."

Max lifted Lydia to the ground. She wondered if she'd ever get used to his strength.

She smoothed her skirt and then hurried up to the house.

"Hello. How may I help you?"

All of the people started talking at once.

Lydia waved her arms up and down. "Please. One at a time." She pointed at a woman at the head of the line. "You first."

"My name is Zelda Polenski and I have a sick cat. She won't eat and I'm afraid she's dying. I heard that you might be able to help her."

Lydia looked at the gray cat, saw her distended belly and saw movement there. She immediately knew the cat was expecting. "Mrs. Polenski. Your cat is not sick. She's expecting and, by the look of her, she's probably getting ready to deliver soon. They often stop eating at this time. Take her home, make her a warm bed with some old towels and you'll probably have kittens in the morning."

The woman's eyes got big. "Oh, no. That situation can't be. My husband will kill the kittens and then beat me for letting the cat get in a family way. You have to keep her. Please."

Lydia couldn't let the poor woman be beaten. She'd like Max to have a word with the husband, but he'd probably just take it out on his poor wife.

"All right. I'll keep her." She took the cat from Zelda who hurried away. "Max would you put her inside, please. She can go in the raccoon's box since Bandit's never in it anyway." She looked at the line of people. "Next."

She spent the next hour talking to people about their animals. In addition to the pregnant cat she ended up with an ailing dog, a goat and a pig. She helped two other people give aid to their animals, which weren't seriously ill.

Lydia recognized the last visitor who held a bundle wrapped in towels. "Why, Miss Bullock, how are you?"

"I'm fine Mrs. Caldwell and I married the man who promised to wed me. His name is Rafferty. Seamus Rafferty."

"Well, Mrs. Rafferty, what can I do for you and what do you have all wrapped up?"

The woman unwrapped the towels enough for Lydia to see she held a very young fawn.

"My husband shot this little ones mother before he realized she had a fawn. It's not the right season for young one's you see, so he had no idea. We don't have any way to raise it or anywhere to keep it. Can you help? I'd hate to see it die."

Lydia took the fawn in her arms. The little female was very small…maybe a week old. She'd have to hand-raise this one. She'd need to get several baby bottles from the mercantile. The nipples were difficult to clean and would have to be replaced often so the baby didn't sicken from unsanitary milk. But she could certainly afford to do the task.

Max stayed outside with her unless he was taking an animal inside. She had him put them in the kitchen and with the door closed so they couldn't wander the house, at least until they were examined and added to the existing menagerie.

When Lydia went into the kitchen she was greeted by chaos.

"Max," she shouted over the cacophony of sounds. "They don't like each other."

He cocked his head and frowned. "I can see that."

"Open the kitchen door so they can go out into the enclosure."

She was so happy Joe and Max had built the enclosure. The structure was a place where her animals could get fresh air without being loosed upon the populace.

As the goat and piglet joined her animals outside, she was left with the baby fawn and the pregnant cat.

First she checked on the cat lying in Bandit's box behind the stove. As Lydia had suspected, she was in hard labor and one kitten was almost out. She watched until the kitten was born and the mama cat cleaned off the birthing sack. Seeing that the cat had everything well in hand, she got a wash cloth and then heated milk on the stove.

"Max, would you go to the mercantile and get me four baby bottles? I'll start this fawn on the milk letting her suck on a wash cloth but I don't think she'll get enough that way. She needs a bottle."

"I'm on my way. Will you be all right while I'm gone?"

"Yes, I'll be fine."

About fifteen minutes after he left, the cat started howling.

When Lydia looked down into the box, she knew the cat was in trouble.

Chapter 13

Lydia realized the mother cat was having a breech birth. This event wasn't uncommon in cats, but if she didn't get that kitten out the rest of the litter could die while waiting to be born.

She very gently grasped the kitten and pulled slowly, just giving the mother cat a little help in expelling the kitten from her body. As Lydia pulled the mama pushed, and with both of their efforts the kitten was born. The mama cat licked the sack from the kittens face and the tiny baby meowed in response. The sound was so soft Lydia almost didn't hear it.

Max had returned and stood behind her, out of the way. "That was amazing. Where did you learn how to do that and not hurt the cat?"

Lydia turned and looked up at Max.

"I just knew. I've done it before, but the first time pulling a kitten or a puppy was just instinct."

"Well, you did great." He pointed at the cat. "Look, there's another kitten."

Sure enough the mama cat birthed another kitten and then another.

Lydia sat back on her heels from her kneeling position. "Oh my, eight kittens in all. They will be terrors when they get old enough to climb out of the box. We'll have to watch where we step."

He helped her stand.

"What will you do with the piglet and the baby goat?"

She walked to the counter where he'd put the sack of supplies and took out the bottles and nipples. "Well, the piglet is the runt and the mother didn't have enough teats for thirteen piglets, that's why we got him."

"Will you keep him as a pet or raise him for slaughter?"

She whipped her head around. "Never for slaughter! How can you suggest such a thing?" She ate meat and so did her babies, but she also knew she would never send her pets to be turned into bacon.

Max held up his hands. "I'm sorry. I should have known better."

"Well, now you do."

She watched the mother cat a little longer to make sure all eight babies found a teat. Once she was certain, she washed her hands with water from the bucket on the stove.

Then she checked the goat and the piglet, to confirm they were healthy. The one she worried about was the baby deer. She got a towel and wrapped the fawn before setting her by the stove to keep warm.

Now she had to make a mother's milk substitute. She took a cup of cow's milk, the yolk of one egg and a half teaspoon of sugar dissolved in water, mixed it together well and put it in the baby bottle. She used a knife to widen the hole in the nipple for the fawn, and for other large animal babies.

She sat on the floor and took the fawn in her arms, holding the bottle high to mimick the mama deer. The little thing was almost too weak to nurse, but once she got started she seemed to remember how and the bottle was finished in no time.

Lydia refilled the bottle and repeated the process.

Max seemed content to sit and watch her.

"You'll make a great mother," he said out of the blue.

"I hope so. I'm looking forward to being a mother."

"You know that can only happen when we have relations."

"I know and I've gotten to know you since we married. I'm used to sleeping with you and cuddling with you. I think I'm ready to make love to you."

She looked up in time to see his jaw drop.

Lydia chuckled. "Close your mouth, Max, you'll catch flies."

He cleared his throat. "We can do so tonight, if you'd like. Joe and Hannah are gone. John is at the opposite end of the hall and Hetty is downstairs. The arrangement gives about as much privacy as we can hope for."

She smiled. "I know. That's another reason I want to make love tonight."

Hetty entered from the living room having returned from seeing her sister, another bride from the wagon train. She was a pretty girl, about as tall as Lydia, with shiny, brown hair pulled straight back into a bun high on her forehead. "Holy cow! Look at all these animals." She grinned. "I think I must have died and gone to heaven."

Lydia laughed. "I'm glad you think so. Why don't you get that baby goat outside and bottle feed him? You can make him a version of mother's milk." She gave Hetty the recipe.

Hetty went to work making a batch of the milk, gathered the goat in a towel like Lydia had the fawn and fed the little kid.

"Well, Max. You can try to catch the piglet." She jutted her chin toward the door to the enclosure. "He'll need feeding too. He's too young to be eating solid food yet. He can't be more than about five weeks old."

"I'll catch the little guy and then we'll all be feeding babies."

Before they made love, she wanted him to realize this is how it would always be. Controlled chaos. "This chaos is my life, Max. If you can't deal with it, you better get out now because I don't intend to change."

He shook his head. "I'm not going anywhere. When we married, I vowed for better or for worse." Then he smiled. "I think I can put up with a few animals."

She looked around the kitchen at all the creatures. "This isn't a few and we'll get more now that I've taken in these. People will bring their animals. Which reminds me, a friend of Doc Wade's will be bringing his dog who is about to have puppies. People will bring me injured wild animals probably babies, because full grown animals don't tend to get caught. They usually die instead. I want to buy the land behind and on both sides of us. Can you check and see who owns it for me? Then we'll make them an offer."

"Sure, but I bet, since no building's there, you already own it."

"If that's the case, I want to build a barn and a corral on one side for the large animals and another enclosure, a shed surrounded with high chicken wire for the smaller ones, in the summer anyway. The weather is too cold right now for the little ones to be out there at night."

"I'll see to all of those things, beginning tomorrow."

"Thank you." She looked down at the fawn now full and sleeping. Such a little one to be without her mother. Lydia left her wrapped in the towel and laid her by the stove.

The rest of the afternoon was spent feeding and examining the new arrivals. Lydia hummed or sang the entire time. The kittens were three toms and five girls. Hopefully she could find them good homes when they were about eight weeks old, more than likely with the new brides who came in on the wagon train.

Lydia stopped long enough to prepare dinner. She was anxious to get all the feedings done, human and animal. Max was more than ready but had been very patient with her. She realized she wanted children, human babies of her own. As much as she loved her animals, raising them wasn't the same.

After dinner she helped Hetty with the dishes.

Max and John fed the older orphans, while she and Hetty sat on the floor and bottle fed the littlest babies. Finally all were down for the night.

"I'm exhausted," said Lydia. "I'm headed for bed."

"Right behind you," said Max.

Lydia stood. "Goodnight, Hetty, John. See you in the morning."

"Sleep well," said John.

"See you at midnight," said Hetty.

"We'll be here," said Max. "Goodnight to you both."

Lydia led the way to the bedroom, as she did every night. This time, when she entered the bedroom, instead of going to the closet and changing into a nightgown, she waited for Max to close the door and come to her.

He didn't disappoint. Max took her in his arms and kissed her hard.

She wrapped her arms around his neck and held on.

He lifted her and walked to the bed, his lips never leaving hers.

"Are you sure, Lydia? I don't want to push you into something you don't want yet."

"I'm sure. I want babies, Max. Lots of babies." *I want to show you how much I love you even if you don't love me.*

He kissed her softly and set her feet on the floor. Then he unbuttoned her blouse, grazing her skin above her chemise with his fingers. When the fastenings were all open, he pushed the blouse down her arms and onto the floor.

Taking her cue from him, she unbuttoned his shirt and pushed it off his arms. He was magnificent. She couldn't stop herself running her hands over his hard muscle.

He unbuttoned her skirt and let it pool around her feet then he pulled the ribbon on her chemise, watching as it fell open.

Embarrassed she wanted to reach up and pull her chemise together, but seeing the smile on Max's face she resisted. She wasn't really sure what to do now that his shirt was off. She didn't feel right removing his pants like he did her skirt.

"Lydia? What's wrong?"

"I…I can't remove your pants. It doesn't feel—"

"Shh." He put two fingers over her lips. "That's fine. I'll remove them when I finish with your clothes. Is that all right with you?"

She nodded, her stomach in knots. What if her body wasn't as pretty as Anna's? What if he wasn't pleased with her?

Max removed her chemise and then her bloomers before making quick work of his own clothing.

When they were both naked, he pulled down the bedcovers, picked her up and laid her in the middle of the mattress. He came down beside her and braced himself on one elbow. Using his free hand he ran a finger along her collar bones, in-between her breasts, and then under and around them before coming to rest on her nipple.

Lydia lay stiff as a board, her breathing shallow. She was suddenly scared, not of Max. She loved him, but feared the act, knowing there would be pain.

"Lydia, I won't hurt you. You're my wife. Hurting you is not something I desire to do. I want you to feel as much pleasure as possible."

"There is pleasure? I never believed the rumors I heard that that was the reason my father and aunt were supposed to be having an affair."

"Yes. Didn't your mother tell you about your wedding night?"

Lydia shook her head.

"What about Hannah? Hasn't she…explained things?"

"I never asked and she didn't volunteer the information."

"I see. Well, let me tell you what is about to happen."

She shook her head again. "I've been around animals all my life and have an idea about the mechanics, but I wanted to know if there will be pain. You said there is pleasure which is unexpected, I admit."

"This first time there will be some pain because you are untried, being a virgin."

"But, I don't want there to be pain. It frightens me."

"I'll make sure to prepare you as much as I can to minimize the pain, and next time we make love you'll have no pain. You'll feel only desire and joy. I promise."

She let out a whoosh of air. "So no pleasure this time—"

He stroked a hand up and down her arm to calm her. "No, you'll enjoy it this time as well. That's the part where I prepare you. You'll have pleasure then."

"Very well," She put her arms at her sides and looked at the ceiling. "I'm ready."

Max chuckled. "Darlin', relax. Remember, I'll make you feel wonderful. Just feel, don't think... feel."

Lydia took a deep breath and willed her body to relax.

Max touched her.

She shivered, wanting nothing more than for him to continue. As though he could read her thoughts, he stroked her arms and between her breasts. He squeezed them gently and rubbed her nipples until they stood hard as rocks. Then he moved down her body to her mound.

"Oh, Max. My God, please tell me there's more."

"There's definitely more, my sweet. We've only just begun."

He leaned down and kissed her, then pleasured her until she started to scream as her body shattered and she rose to the heavens. Max caught her sounds with his kiss.

Then he covered her and made love to her, slowly and sweetly.

If Lydia hadn't been in love with Max before, she was now. He'd taken great care of her. Treated her tenderly, with reverence, and what she felt was love.

He kept her with him as he rolled to his back, tucking her safely into his side. Then he pulled the blankets over them and fell to sleep.

Lydia couldn't sleep. She had so many thoughts going through her head, chief among them the question of whether they'd made a baby tonight. If not, how long before they did?

Horace Belcher didn't run far. He'd found an abandoned cabin deep in the woods north of Oregon City. He had the diamonds, but he needed cash until he could get to a large enough city and to a jeweler who'd buy the uncut gems. He knew Walter had kept cash in the safe in his house, which meant the woman had it now, too. He'd stayed away, hoping they thought he was gone and their defenses were down, but now was the time.

He had to have the money. He deserved it, after putting up with Walter for almost a year. His plan would have worked out if Walter hadn't left everything to Lydia Granger. His bride. He'd poisoned Walter for nothing.

His death didn't matter. Horace would get the money. All of it. Or his name wasn't…Horace Belcher. He laughed.

Chapter 14

Tuesday, January 4, 1853

The next day, Horace watched the house. She always seemed to have someone there with her. He really wanted her alone, but he finally decided he could handle both women if he had to.

The cabin he was staying in was cold. He'd found it quite by accident on one of his excursions looking for such a place where he could hide out.

After his trip to the Wagon's Ho Saloon while in disguise, he knew everyone expected him to go to the coast and catch a ship to San Francisco. He would eventually do that, but he would go to Seattle not Portland to board the ship. That choice would be unexpected, but less dangerous and gave him the opportunity to get the rest of the money.

His vigilance paid off Thursday morning, two days later. That Walsh Detective agent and the other man left the house, leaving just the two women. Horace didn't know how long the men would be gone, so he ran to the house, knowing he had to hurry and rob it so he could make a clean getaway. He worked his way around to the back of the house but had forgotten they had built a huge pen for the silly woman's pets.

Everyone in town knew she wouldn't turn away an animal and brought her every sick, unwanted, or abandoned critter they could find. She had to have more than a dozen by now.

Blocked by the pen, he went back around to the front and knocked on the door. Then he pulled out his pistol and waited.

The young woman with brown hair answered the door.

Horace pointed his revolver at her. "Take me to Miss Granger. Oh, I mean Mrs. Caldwell." He waved the Colt at her. "Now."

The girl raised her hands. "Please don't shoot."

"If you don't move, you *will* die and I'll find her anyway when she comes running to find out what the shot was." He waved the gun again. "Now move."

The girl turned and walked toward the back of the house toward, as he knew from his many visits with Walter, the kitchen.

She went through the door and he pushed her into the room. "No stalling."

The young woman stumbled.

"Hetty? What's the—"

Lydia Caldwell stood at the counter, a large knife in one hand and a mountain of raw meat piled on a cutting board beside her.

"Put down the knife, Lydia and...Hetty, is that what you called her? Yes, Hetty won't get hurt."

Lydia set down the knife. She dropped her hand to her skirt and felt the gun in her pocket, but she didn't want Hetty to be hurt.

"Good girl. Now, you'll open the safe in Walter's office if you want this pretty young thing to remain that way."

Lydia raised her chin. "The money won't do you any good. Max will find you. You killed his wife, the only woman he's ever loved. He'll follow you to the ends of the earth."

"But he won't find me. Look how long I've been hiding out, two weeks and he still hasn't found me. He won't find me now, either. So get moving." He waved the gun at Hetty. "Or do I have to kill her before you believe me."

"No! I'll get you the money. Follow me."

Lydia instinctively placed a hand on her side where her wound was and took him to Walter's office where the huge safe stood solitary in the empty room. She knew her time was limited and he would kill them when he got the money. She had to do something, but she didn't want to endanger Hetty, or herself for that matter.

"Don't dawdle. Open that safe now," said Belcher from behind her.

"Why would I delay? I want you out of here as soon as possible." She walked to the safe and put in the combination, then pulled the handle. Nothing. Why couldn't she open the darn safe without having to try again and again?

He waved the gun at her. "What did you do? I said open the safe."

"I'm trying." She pointed at him. "I'm a little nervous with you waving that gun around."

"If you don't open that safe, I'll shoot the girl now but I won't kill her. I'll shoot first one leg and then somewhere else if you miss again. We'll keep doing that until you get the safe open. Do you understand me?"

"Yes. I understand." Hands shaking, she very slowly put in the combination and remembered to do the last turn three times *before* stopping on the number. She grabbed the handle and pulled. The safe opened.

Belcher looked inside and whistled. "Walter had even more money here than in the bank."

She wrinkled her brow and narrowed her eyes. "Perhaps he had reason not to put everything in the bank."

The murderer, former bank president, and current robber gave a single laugh. "Like he could figure out who I was. Is that what you think? Well, he didn't, because he still let me into the house and allowed me to fix our drinks. As soon as the poison started working, I pestered him to tell me the combination to the safe, but he wouldn't do it. Apparently he'd already written up his will leaving everything to you."

Lydia knew she and Hetty were in grave danger. Lydia's suspicions were confirmed, but both she and Hetty could now implicate him for the murder. He had no choice but to kill them if he wanted to get away.

She heard the approaching click of Sampson's nails on the hardwood floors.

"Sampson!" She pointed at the intruder. "Attack!"

The nearly full-grown wolf bared his teeth and ran at Belcher.

The man turned in time to fire off one round.

The bullet glanced off Sampson's shoulder but didn't slow him. He jumped and bit into Belcher's gun arm.

Screaming in pain, the would-be-robber dropped his pistol. It hit the floor with a clunk, and in his effort to get the wolf off of him, he accidentally kicked the gun toward Lydia.

She bent and picked up the pistol, pointing it at Belcher.

Horace kept screaming and hitting Sampson with his left hand, but the animal wouldn't release his arm.

Sampson shook his head and buried his teeth farther into the man's flesh.

"Sampson. Here boy." Lydia said softly, patting her leg.

The wolf shook Belcher a couple more times before releasing him and sitting next to Lydia, his gaze focused on the murderer.

She kept the gun leveled. "You never should have threatened me. Sampson is very protective."

"I should have killed the animal like I did Walter," spat Belcher.

Footsteps pounded down the hallway and then Max burst into the room with John right behind.

"We heard a gunshot." Max, his gaze quickly took in the scene. He hurried to Belcher then.

Max looked over at Lydia. "If you're all right, I need the scarf from your blouse."

She handed John the gun and quickly untied the material from around her neck to give to Max.

He took the long length of silk and made quick work of binding Belcher's hands behind his back and then forcing him to his knees. "Stay there if you want to live." Then he took the man's belt and tied his ankles together.

Belcher grumbled and then sat back on his heels.

Sampson matched her steps keeping to her side. The wolf growled at Belcher and bared his teeth.

Lydia knelt next to her pet. "Sampson! You wonderful wolf. You saved my life and now you're hurt. Mama will fix you up in no time." She looked up at Max. "I'm fine. Sampson saved me." She jutted her chin toward Belcher. "He would have killed me after he took all the money, and Hetty too."

Lydia stood and walked to Max. "I've never been so glad to see someone in my life." She threw her arms around his neck. "I'm not sure I could have shot him, even to save myself."

Max wrapped her in his embrace and held her tight. "You're all right now. I'm here. I'll never let anything harm you if I can help it."

Finally feeling safe in his arms, she didn't move away from him. "Thank you."

He pulled back and looked at her. "I didn't do anything. You and Sampson had the situation well in hand. I can't believe now, that I thought keeping a wolf was a bad thing." Max released Lydia, so he could bend down and scratch Sampson behind the ears. "You are a very good boy. Now, I'll let your mama fix you up." Max looked up at Lydia. "Will he be okay?"

"Yes. I'm pretty sure he will be." She turned and headed for the kitchen. "Come, boy." Lydia patted her thigh. "Let's go get you cleaned up and give you an extra portion of meat."

Max followed them. "He deserves two."

Lydia smiled and nodded. "Yes, he does." She stopped and jutted her chin toward Belcher. "Shouldn't we watch him?"

Max looked at Belcher. "He should be fine. His arm is injured and he can't get up from there without using his arms with his ankles tied."

"Are you sure you're all right?" John asked Hetty. "Maybe you should lie down for a while."

Hetty reached up and cupped his face. "I'm fine. Thank you for caring."

His hand covered hers. "I do care. I don't want to see anything happen to you."

"Nothing will happen to me."

Lydia smiled and whispered to Max. "It would appear your young friend is smitten with our Hetty."

Max stood behind Lydia and wrapped his arms around her waist. "If he's smart, he'll marry her fast and not let her get away."

Lydia stepped forward out of his arms. "I must treat Sampson."

Max didn't try to pull her back. "Of course. I should get the sheriff."

Lydia took Max's hand. "Belcher timed it so you and John were gone. He knew he couldn't take you on. There was nothing you could have done that would have made the outcome any different."

"I still feel like I should have protected you."

"We didn't know. He's been gone for two weeks, but now you have to question him and find the diamonds."

"I'm going now."

A knock sounded from the front door.

Max turned toward the front of the house. "I'll get it."

Max opened the door.

"Daddy!" Julia shouted as she ran toward him.

"Julia." Max knelt and opened his arms. He hadn't been so happy since he'd married Lydia. "Baby."

She hugged him around the neck.

His arms encircled his little daughter and he buried his face in her hair, drinking in her scent, like a man about to die of thirst. He stood and looked over at his brother-in-law, sister-in-law and nephew. "Roy. Gwen. Thank you so much for bringing her to me. I have a situation that I need to take care of. It would be best if you went to the hotel for now until I handle it. I shall return after I escort him to the sheriff's office."

"I don't think you will," said Roy.

"Why is that?"

"I assume he's the man running away from the house with his wrists tied behind his back," said Gwen.

"What?!" Max ran from the room.

CHAPTER 15

Entering the living room with John and Hetty, Lydia turned to them. "Please watch the children. The animals won't hurt them. Nonetheless it's probably best to wait until I return and can introduce them." She didn't wait for an answer but hurried after Max.

Lydia saw Max slam the door shut and hurried after him. She felt the weight of her pistol in her pocket right where it was supposed to be. This time if she ran into Belcher, she would shoot, no questions asked. She pulled the weapon.

As they reached town, she took the time to check each street and alley before she passed. Lydia didn't want the man getting the drop on her.

Max headed straight to the sheriff's office.

She knew if they could comb the town and surrounding area now, they had a better chance of finding him.

From the alley just past the butcher shop, Belcher jumped out behind Max. He held a heavy, club like stick in his left hand and hit Max on the back of the head with it, knocking him out cold.

"Max!"

Lydia ran at Belcher, firing the gun, just as he disarmed Max.

She missed.

Belcher looked up and gave her an evil grin as he used his left hand to aim the revolver at her husband's head.

Lydia's mouth went dry. The sight of Belcher threatening her husband made her vision focus only on Belcher's body. She fired again.

She hit Belcher in the stomach.

He flinched and bent over.

She adjusted her aim and fired again, hitting his left shoulder. The gun fell from his hand.

Using his injured right arm he picked up the weapon and again aimed it at Max.

Lydia was only about fifteen feet away when she fired a fourth time. This time, the bullet hit him in the heart, and he collapsed on top of Max. When she reached them, she pushed off Belcher without as much as a second glance.

"Max. Max." She patted his cheeks.

His head was bleeding profusely.

She ripped the bottom on her petticoat and pressed the cloth to the wound as she heard boots pounding toward her.

Sheriff McCauley knelt beside her.

"Lydia. Let me take him to Doc Wade."

She nodded and stepped back so the sheriff could pick up Max.

The sheriff knelt next to Max. "Jed, help me pick up this man and get him over my shoulder."

"What about him?" Lydia pointed at Belcher. "I don't want anyone touching him until Max gets a chance to examine him."

The sheriff jutted his chin toward another deputy. "You heard her Roscoe. You and Jed get him to the undertaker with the instructions to hold off on the burial for a day. Max should be able to see to him by then."

Lydia nodded. "He admitted he murdered Walter. Said he poisoned him."

"I always wondered, because Walt was in good shape for a man of sixty-one. I never expected him to drop dead."

When they reached the doctor's office, Lydia held the door open so Robert could bring in Max.

"Doc Wade! Are you here?" shouted the sheriff.

The doctor walked out of the back room. "Good grief. No need to yell. I'm here. Who do you have there?"

"Max Caldwell."

"He was hit over the head with a club," said Lydia. She wrung her hands, the sight of so much blood worrying her.

Max stirred.

"He's waking up, Doc. Where do you want him?"

Doc turned and went back from whence he came. "Follow me."

Robert carried Max in and laid him on the table in the center of the room. The table held a small mattress covered by a sheet.

Lydia remembered being on that same table after Belcher shot her. Now, seeing Max there, she felt worse than if it had been her back on the table. She hated seeing him hurt and would gladly change places with him. Were these feelings part of what love was? Wanting to take the pain for the person you loved so they didn't feel it?

She wasn't sure, not of anything. Right now, all she felt was anger toward the man she'd killed for hurting the man she loved.

"Let me up. I'm fine."

Max's voice brought her out of her reverie.

Doc Wade pushed Max back onto the table. "Will you lie still so I can examine you, please?"

"Max." She touched his hand.

At her touch and the sound of her voice, he stopped moving.

"Let the doctor examine you. Then we can go inspect Belcher's body. I don't believe he left those diamonds in a room or hideout. He's got them on him and we have to find where."

"You're right." Max furrowed his brows. "Okay, Doc, get on with it."

"Very well. Follow my finger." The doctor moved his finger right and then left in front of Max. "Good. Open your eyes wide." Doc Wade held open Max's eyelid and checked his eyes. "Your pupils are dilated, not unexpected after a conk on the head. You might have a concussion, so I want Lydia to keep an eye on you. I don't want you to sleep for at least four hours and I want Lydia to wake you every two hours after that."

"I'll do that, Doctor," said Lydia. "Is he released to leave now?"

"Yes, yes. Go." The doctor looked at Max. "No heavy lifting of any kind. I suggest you take the sheriff with you to examine that body."

"Sure thing. I'll go home and relax after our inspection, but I won't sleep for four hours, I promise."

"Good."

"Goodbye, Doctor," said Lydia.

"Thanks. And send us the bill for this visit, please." Max put his hand at Lydia's waist and guided her out of the building. "Okay, let's go see what secrets Belcher is hiding. Robert, are you coming?"

"Wouldn't miss it."

The three of them hurried out.

Lydia didn't like going to the undertaker. There was something unnerving about it. But when she got there, she discovered it was just a simple shop with a small room in the front to greet mourners and the workroom with the bodies in the back.

"We'd like to see the body of Horace Belcher," said Max.

"Right this way." The tall, gaunt man had Belcher laid out on a table in a back room. He'd apparently followed the sheriff's instructions and hadn't touched the body.

Lydia began unbuttoning the man's coat. "I'll check his clothes. You take off his boots. Check the heels. One might be hollow."

Max cocked a brow. "You seem to know an awful lot about hiding places for gems."

"I've had to sew money into the hems of our dresses or coats. We had to hide it from our landlords, so we could eat. They can take your coat, but they can't take the dress you're wearing and leave you naked."

"No, I don't suppose they couldn't."

Max pulled off Belcher's right boot. When he tried to pull off the left, the heel came loose in his hand.

"Well, what do we have here?" He held up a small bag, like a cloth tobacco pouch.

Lydia grinned. "Told you. It's the diamonds."

"I bet you're right." He opened the bag and poured the contents into his hand.

A pile of dull stones looking more like quartz than diamonds poured out.

"Robert, you are a witness that we found these on Horace Belcher, real name Gilbert Ross. Do you have any objection to us putting these into the safe until I determine their disposition?"

Robert shook his head. "None. That's the safest place in town other than the bank and since Lydia owns that business anyway, I see no difference."

Max nodded, put the diamonds back into the bag and then slipped it into his pocket. He held out his hand to her. "Shall we go home?"

"Yes." She took his hand, glanced at his bandaged head and was grateful he wasn't hurt worse. As they walked back home, she broached the question she wasn't sure she wanted the answer to. "Will you be taking them back to Chicago yourself?"

"I don't know yet. I've got a couple of ideas, but I won't say until I get some answers. Are you unhappy that the money Belcher spent won't be recovered? I'm sure we'll find the money he took in his saddlebags and that he left his horse at the livery. He wouldn't have wanted it to be out on the street where anyone could steal it."

"All right. I'm not worried about that. I'm worried about you leaving. I'll be honest and tell you that I hope you don't go, but I also understand you have to do your job."

Max nodded. "Yes, there is that."

"What about Julia? Will you leave her here while you go back?"

"Since I don't know for sure that I'm leaving, I won't answer that question. As I said, I have an idea but I need answers first."

They walked the rest of the way home in silence. Lydia went immediately to the safe and put in the diamonds. Then she went back to the living room.

John was playing host to Roy James and his family.

John and Roy both stood as Lydia and Max entered.

"Hetty is feeding the animals," said John.

Lydia nodded as she stood next to Max. "Oh, good. I wondered where she was."

"So Roy," said Max. "Tell me how you found me."

"We went to the sheriff's office and inquired to your whereabouts. He said you live here with your wife. I hadn't realized you married again…so soon."

Roy's tone left Max feeling like he'd been slapped in the face, but he understood the man's position. Anna was his sister and had only been gone for about eighteen months.

"It's a long story." He took Lydia's hand and brought it to his lips. "This is my wife Lydia. My dear, these two are Roy and Gwen James and the little boy is their son Billy."

"I'm pleased to make your acquaintance. Max told me how you have taken care of Julia for him. We are both so grateful."

"You'll have to forgive us for running out as we did," said Max. "We had to get the man that killed

Anna. As you can see, it was a struggle, but he's dead. Lydia shot him and saved my life."

Lydia leaned into Max's side. "We'd never have caught him the first time if it hadn't been for Sampson, my pet wolf."

"You caught him?" Roy's eyes widened as what Lydia said sunk in. "Pet. Wolf?"

Max nodded. "I know what you're thinking, but he's gentle as can be when he's not protecting the family. Follow me. We'll get you some refreshment, you can tell us about your trip and you can meet our family."

Lydia was so pleased when her husband referred to her babies as their family. Her heart was overflowing with love for this wonderful man she'd married.

As they walked toward the back of the house, Simba and Trinity barreled by. Simba was chasing Trinity but seemed to be making sure not to catch the kitten too soon.

Gwen's eyes widened. "Was that a three-legged cat being chased by a…a…mountain lion?"

"Yes," said Max, without slowing down.

"Kitties," said Julia and wiggled to get out of her father's arms.

"You can play with the kitties in a little bit. I want you to meet someone first, Sugar Pie."

Julia giggled. "I not sugar pie. I Julia."

Max laughed. "Yes, you are Julia. My little sweetie."

She nodded and hugged her father around the neck.

They walked into the kitchen where Hetty was picking up the food plates, all the animals done with their meal. She looked around as they came in and gave a little squeal before clasping her fingers over her lips.

She hugged Lydia. "I'm so glad you are all right." She turned to Max. "You must be Julia. I'm so pleased to meet you."

Julia ignored her and wiggled in her daddy's hold. "Doggie!"

"Can she pet Sampson? Will she hurt him?" asked Max.

"Of course, she can pet him. He'll love it. I'll show her how not to hurt him."

Max set Julia down and she ran to Sampson throwing her arms around the big wolf's neck.

"Doggie," she said as she buried her face in his neck.

Sampson simply sat there and let the little girl hug him.

"Everyone have a seat and I'll get us coffee along with cookies I baked yesterday."

Roy helped Gwen into a chair.

Billy was watching Julia with Sampson his thumb in his mouth.

Looking over at him, Lydia sighed. "Is he afraid of animals?"

"Not usually," said Gwen. "But your wolf is a big animal and he might find him intimidating."

Lydia went over to the little boy. "Would you like to pet him, too?"

He nodded.

"Come with me." She took his hand with her left hand and they walked over to Julia and Sampson.

Lydia squatted in front of her pet. "Billy, this is Sampson. You can pet him if you like. He likes children. See how he lets Julia hug him?"

The little boy nodded and stepped closer to Sampson and patted him on the head between his ears.

Sampson licked Billy's face.

He giggled and hugged him like Julia was.

Lydia chuckled. "Sampson seems to be very happy with your little ones."

"We're happy to be here as well," said Roy. "Though we're surprised to find Max remarried."

Lydia's smile never faltered. "We were somewhat surprised ourselves. You see Max compromised me and then had to marry me. It's a long story and one of many we'll tell you at supper tonight."

Julia came in just as she was closing the safe.

"Lydia?" The little girl stood swaying back and forth with her hands behind her back. Uncle Roy say I no play with Simba unless you play too. Will ya? Huh?"

Lydia laughed. "Of course, I will. Come on. Let's get you acquainted with Simba and Trinity. They are best friends and I want you to be their friend, too. That means you have to learn how to play with them."

"Okay." She put her thumb in her mouth.

Lydia gently tugged Julia's hand until the offending digit popped out of her mough. "What would your daddy say?"

The child hung her head. "No suck thumb."

"That's right. You're a big girl now and big girls don't suck their thumbs."

Julia frowned. "I no wanna be big girl."

"Because you want to suck your thumb?"

She nodded. "And Daddy loved me when I was a little girl."

Lydia's heart broke and she opened her arms. "Ah, sweetie."

Julia ran into her arms.

"Your daddy loves you very much."

"But he go away. He not love me. Aunt Gwen said so."

Lydia's anger at the callousness of the woman almost boiled over. She would not have this baby's head filled with fear.

She hugged Julia just a little tighter. The tiny girl might not be her child by birth, but she would be by wanting and caring and loving.

"Let's go find the kittens and then I'm having a little talk with Aunt Gwen."

Twenty minutes later Lydia knocked on the door to the bedroom she'd given Roy and Gwen while they stayed at her home.

"Come in," Gwen called.

Lydia entered, finding Gwen lying on the bed reading a book. She lifted a brow. "I thought you were indisposed and resting."

Gwen put aside the book. "I am resting. Reading is what I do when I rest. Finding the time to read with a husband and child is difficult. But then you wouldn't know that, having acquired your husband just a short time ago."

"On the contrary. I read every night before Max comes to bed. Perhaps that is what you should do." She waved her hand. "That is not what I came here to talk to you about."

Gwen cocked a brow. "Yes. Why have you come?"

Lydia fisted her hands at her side. "I want you to stop filling Julia's head with nonsense. I want you to stop telling her that her father doesn't love her. You don't know Max at all if you believe he feels anything but the greatest love for her. He has missed her more than you can ever imagine."

Gwen rose from the bed. "If that were the case he never would have left her."

"He had a job to do and you know he had no choice. I would bet that Roy has no idea what you've done."

"What has she done?" Roy asked from the hall behind Lydia.

She spun around, narrowed her gaze and swung out her hand pointing at Gwen. "Your wife has been telling Julia that Max doesn't love her because, if he did, he wouldn't have left. He thought he was leaving Julia with people who loved her, where she would be safe. Now I wonder if he didn't make a mistake."

Roy narrowed his eyes and glared at his wife. "Is this true?"

Gwen straightened her back and raised her chin a notch. "Yes, it's true. And I haven't changed my mind. If he'd loved her, he'd have stayed in Chicago and we wouldn't have taken this God-forsaken trip here to bring her to him. I've never been so miserable in my life. Why shouldn't I spread the feeling?"

Roy's gaze never left his wife. "Lydia, would you excuse us? And would you please keep an eye on Billy and see that he doesn't come up here?"

Lydia nodded. "Certainly."

As she left she heard Roy yell, "What the hell were you thinking? What's the matter with you, that you would be so cruel?"

She knew she shouldn't eavesdrop so she hurried away from the door, but she didn't feel the least bit sorry for Gwen.

Later at dinner, Gwen acted very subdued. She kept her gaze on her plate and mostly pushed around the food, with a bite or two now and then.

Eventually, she rose. "I hope you'll excuse me. I've a headache and need to lie down."

Max, Roy and John all stood as she left the room.

When they were reseated, Lydia turned toward Roy. "I hope she's not becoming ill. Should we call for the doctor?"

He shook his head. "I'm sure she'll be fine."

Lydia felt no niggle of guilt for what she may have caused. Gwen deserved everything she got for being so cruel to Julia. "Well, if she's not better tomorrow, she should see the doctor."

"Of course." He put his napkin beside his plate. "I'd best check on her. Excuse me."

Lydia returned her attention to her plate, but found she suddenly had no appetite either.

Max gazed at her and narrowed his eyes. "I get the feeling you know more about Gwen's headache than you've said."

"Perhaps. We'll discuss it later."

John and Hetty stood.

"If you don't mind, Hetty and I are taking a walk now. We'll bundle up against the brisk air."

"Don't blame you," Max stood.

After they'd left he reseated himself.

"Now we are alone. The children are playing in their room and it's just you and me. What should I know that you haven't told me?"

Lydia took a deep breath. She didn't like telling him something she knew would cause him pain. "Julia told me she didn't want to be a big girl. She wanted to be a little girl so that "Daddy will love me"."

Max frowned. "Of course, I love her. More than just about anything or anyone."

"I know, and that's what I told her. Then I asked why she would think that you don't love her. She said her Aunt Gwen said if you'd loved her you wouldn't have left her."

"Why that—"

"Shh. I know what you're thinking, but such language is not needed here. Besides, I was in the process of telling Gwen when Roy entered the bedroom. He took care of it, but I'm sure that's why she was so restrained at dinner."

Max ran his hands through his hair and paced the kitchen.

"Why would she do something like that? Poison my daughter's mind against me?"

"I don't know. Perhaps she thought she was preparing her if you didn't return or as she told me she was just miserable and resentful, blaming you for them making the trip here."

"I want them to leave. I don't want her around Julia any longer."

Lydia placed her hand on Max's arm as he passed.

Immediately he stopped.

She felt the tension in him and knew she needed to calm him. "They are still your in-laws and they did leave everything behind to come here and bring Julia. Gwen made a mistake—"

"But—"

"Shh. A terrible mistake, but she knows now and she deserves another chance. And you need to spend as much time with Julia as possible." When he would have spoken again, she laid her fingers over his lips and then cupped his jaw. "Give her a chance, Max."

Nodding, he leaned into her hand. "For you, I will. For you, I'd do just about anything. I love you, you know."

She stilled her hand and then pulled away, wrapping both arms around her waist. "You can't just drop something like that on a person. How would I know you love me? You've never said it before." Her voice cracked as tears rolled down her cheeks. "I've known I loved you forever, but I didn't want to make you feel trapped. I wanted you to be able to leave any time you wanted."

Max put his arms around her and pulled her close, trapping her arms between them. "I don't want to go anywhere. I've asked Robert McCauley to return the diamonds and to keep whatever the reward has become, for his trouble in taking them back to Chicago. The amount was two percent of their worth, which was one-hundred-thousand dollars."

Her eyes widened. "Does he know how much it will be?"

"Of course. I couldn't ask him to make the trip without telling him what he could make. I fully expect them to give him closer to five percent when he delivers the stones back to their owner. I didn't tell him that fact though, just in case they don't raise it."

"But who will be the sheriff now?"

"I will, until he returns. John can handle the bank by himself. He doesn't need me."

"What will you do after Robert returns in a year?"

"I'll help you run your shelter for abandoned and injured animals. That's what you want to do, isn't it?"

She nodded. "More than anything."

"Then that work is what we'll do. Walter left you everything he owned. I think he knew you would make good use of the wealth."

Lydia pulled back enough to release her arms which she wrapped around his neck. "I hope he would be happy with what we're doing. I don't really know how he felt about animals. I should ask Robert."

"Yes. Speaking of Walter, I know where he's buried. Would you like to go?"

"I would very much but tomorrow. Now, I want to hear you say it again."

He smiled. "Say what?"

Lydia's mouth turned down. She looked up at him through her lashes. "You know. Say it. Please."

His mouth turned up at one corner. "I love you, Lydia Caldwell. More than anything."

His lips melded with hers in a searing kiss.

She looked forward to a lifetime of kisses, and love and children and animals.

EPILOGUE

Five years later

Lydia stood at the stove stirring the chili she'd just made. Julia and Hannah sat at the table shucking peas. She closed her eyes and pressed her hand against the small of her back as warm liquid flowed down her legs. "Julia."

"Yes, Mama?"

"Please tell your father it's time."

Her daughter's eyes were wide as saucers. "Is the baby coming now?"

She nodded. "I believe it is."

The child ran from the room.

Hannah got up and grabbed a towel.

Lydia lifted her skirt. "My water just broke."

"I can see that." She waved the towel at Lydia.

"I'll wipe this up and you change into a nightdress."

"Of course. Max should be back with the doctor shortly."

"How far apart are your pains?"

"I don't know. I haven't been timing them."

"You go on upstairs. I'll let Joe know he's got to watch all the kids now."

"Max will help when he gets back."

Hannah laughed a single time. "He will not, and you know it. He's just like Joe. Wants to be with you while the baby is born. He likes knowing immediately whether he has a new son or daughter. What do Julia and Benji want?"

"They both would prefer more puppies, but Julia wants a sister and Benji wants a brother."

Lydia walked slowly up the stairs. She stopped halfway when a particularly bad pain hit and she had to bend over and hold her stomach.

If Doc Wade is right, they could each get their wish. I should have told Max that the doctor thought he heard two heart beats, but I didn't want to worry him more than necessary. He already hovered over me just like he did with Benji. If he'd known I could be having twins, he'd have put me to bed for the duration of the pregnancy.

Hannah came in the bedroom carrying towels and a bucket of hot water. "This should be the perfect temperature by the time the doctor gets here."

Lydia started stripping the bed.

"Here let me do that while you get in your nightgown."

It's such a messy business and horribly painful, but having that baby in my arms makes it worth all the pain and mess.

She fluffed the pillows, put them about a foot from the head board and lay down against them. She knew from when Benji was born she needed to be closer to the bottom of the bed where the doctor would stand.

"Mama, Daddy's back!" yelled Julia as she ran into the room.

Doc Wade and Max appeared behind the little girl.

Max went straight to the bed. He took Lydia's hand and stretched out, his long legs on the mattress next to her, his back against the headboard.

"How are you my love?"

She had a nagging ache in her back and couldn't get comfortable, but she said, "I'm fine. Ready for this to be over."

"I bet you are," said Doc Wade. "How long have you been having contractions?"

"They started last night, so about fourteen or fifteen hours. I have a feeling we won't have long to wait." A pain hit her and she squeezed Max's hand as hard as she could until the pain passed. "I'm definitely eager to have this baby."

"Fine. Max, please take Julia downstairs and assist Joe with the youngsters. Hannah will help me now."

"You know that scenario isn't happening, Doc. I don't know why you insist on getting rid of me. Lydia needs me now just like she did three years ago when Benji was born."

The doctor shook his head and sighed. "I don't know what's wrong with you people. You and Joe both seem to feel the need to be where you don't belong."

Max squeezed her hand. "We belong with our wives, with our babies. That's where we belong." He looked over at his daughter. "Julia, sweetheart, you go downstairs and stay with Uncle Joe."

"Okay." She turned and headed toward the door. Halfway there she turned back. "Will Mama be all right?"

Hannah went to Julia. "She'll be just fine and in a little while you'll have a new brother or sister. Now run along and help Uncle Joe with the little ones."

Julia nodded and left the room.

"Thank you, Hannah," said Lydia.

"Anytime. You've done the same for me."

Lydia closed her eyes and moaned. Her back was killing her and all she wanted to do was push. She knew if she could just get the baby out of her body, she'd feel better. "I think this is it, Doc. I need to push."

He stood at the bottom of the bed. "Not yet. Let me look at what we have going on. Raise your knees, please. I know it hurts."

She raised her knees and parted them wide so the doctor could see if the baby was coming or not.

Doc's eyebrows shot up. "Well, I'll be. You're right. I need you to push, Lydia. Now. Push. Push. Push."

She bore down, pushing as hard as she could until she had to rest.

Doc leaned in and positioned his hands to catch the child as it was born. "That's good. Rest. Catch your breath. That's right. Now do it again. Push. Hard. I see the head. Push again."

She felt the baby's head slide out of her body and knew she needed to get the rest of this little one out. She pushed again, hard, and harder still. The baby slid from her.

"You have a beautiful baby girl. Hannah, will you clean up this little one?" He ran his finger around inside the baby's mouth to clear the mucus. The child took her first breath and wailed.

"With pleasure." Hannah carried the baby to the bureau where she laid the tiny girl on a towel and bathed her with a washcloth and water.

"All right now, Lydia. You did wonderfully. Let's do that again."

"A…ag…again!" Max sputtered.

"Lydia?" Doc raised an eyebrow. "Didn't you tell Max you were having twins?"

Max's eyes were round as saucers. "Twins?"

She gazed up at him. "Yes, twins, and this one is anxious to be born. Doc, I don't think we have to wait. It's coming."

Doc grabbed the clean towel next to him. "Okay, push when you can. Let's deliver this baby."

Lydia pushed and then rested twice before the second baby was born. The time was just three minutes after the first.

"This one is a boy. You have two of each now."

Lydia, smiled, content and tired. "And the kids got their wishes granted. A sister for Julia and brother for Benji."

"Hannah, are you ready for this one?" asked Doc. He cleaned his mouth and the baby let out a small squeak.

Hannah brought the baby girl over to the bed and handed her to Lydia. "Here you go, sweet thing. Here's your mama."

As soon as the baby was in her arms, Lydia unwrapped her so she and Max could examine their daughter.

"Look, darlin', she's a redhead. Just like Hannah." Max pointed at his sister-in-law.

"If she's as beautiful she should consider herself blessed." Motherly love burned in Lydia's chest and she raised the baby to her lips and kissed her. She hoped her hair didn't change. She loved the idea of a little Hannah running around the house.

Hannah huffed. "You're just saying that because I'm here in the room. I know you're hoping her hair will change to blonde or brown and it's possible…though not likely. Now, let me get this little guy cleaned up."

A little while later Hannah brought the baby to Max and Lydia.

"I didn't bother swaddling him. You'll just undo it, anyway."

Lydia laughed and gazed at the tiny baby boy. He had brown hair, just like his big sister and daddy. Benji was the only blonde of her children…so far.

Max chuckled. "You're right about that. We have to check them over."

Lydia didn't look up. "That's right and we have to see if their names will fit them."

"What are you naming them?" Hannah asked. "I never could get it out of either of you."

Lydia looked up at Max. "You still agree?"

"I do." He held his daughter, grinning like the proud papa he was.

She turned back to Doc. "We're naming the boy Walter Augustus. We'll call him Walt, Walt Caldwell.

"And the girl?" asked Doc.

"Bonnie because she's a beautiful child. A bonnie lass."

Doc washed up and put away his bag after cleaning his scissors. "Those are good, strong names. Congratulations to both of you."

Max smiled. "Thanks, Doc."

Lydia stared down at her son. She held him and Max held Bonnie.

"Anytime. I'd much rather deal with babies than bullets."

"Never letting us forget that, are you?" asked Max.

"Nope." Doc walked out the door.

"Hannah?" Lydia finally took her gaze off her son. "Will you tell the kids they can come up in about twenty minutes?"

"Sure. We'll all come up together and then you can rest afterward." She followed Doc out.

Max put Bonnie on the bed next to Lydia and then pulled his wife up so she rested her back on the pillows against the headboard. "Why didn't you tell me you were having twins?"

She bit the inside of her lip. "Well, Doc wasn't one hundred percent sure and I didn't want anyone including you to get up your hopes, in case he was wrong. So I kept the possibility to myself. And if he was right, I wanted to surprise you."

He lay down next to her. "Well you certainly did that."

"Forgive me?"

"Of course. Have I told you lately that I love you?"

"I don't think you have."

"Then I've been terribly remiss. I love you, Lydia Caldwell. You're the most amazing woman and I—"

Julia, Benji along with Joey and Letty, Hannah and Joe's kids, burst into the room with their parents on their heels.

"We tried to keep them downstairs but they insisted on coming to meet the newest members of the family," said Joe.

"It's all right," said Lydia. "Max, Hannah, hold the babies so they can see them."

They followed her instructions.

Max showed the children baby Walt. "Well, it looks like all the family is here now."

After a few minutes, the babies started to fuss.

"All right," said Hannah. "Time to go and leave these four alone. The babies need to be fed and Mama and Daddy need some time alone."

She waved her hands and shooed everyone out of the room. At the door Hannah turned back. "You two should be alone for a while now. I'll see everyone stays downstairs."

After everyone left, Max held Bonnie while Lydia opened her nightshirt. Once she got Walt settled and nursing, Max helped her get Bonnie onto the other breast.

When the babies were full, Max and Lydia burped the sleepy infants before laying them on the bed next to their mama.

Lydia gazed down at her tiny children and then up at their father.

"I love you, Max. Thank you for helping make my dreams come true."

"All I did was fall in love with you. Our wedding might not have been the most conventional, but the marriage has definitely worked."

"But marrying to stem gossip is what the Granger women apparently do, since Hannah had to marry Joe the same way."

He chuckled "That's true."

"Did you think we'd ever be this happy?"

He lifted his eyebrows. "When we first got married? To be honest, no, I figured you'd divorce me within the first year."

She took his hand in hers. "I thought the same thing of you, but now I can't fathom us being apart."

He wrapped an arm around her shoulders. "I can't either."

Lydia sighed. "I owe Walter so much. I think he'd be happy we named the baby after him."

Max kissed the top of her head. "I'm sure he would."

"Where are Hetty and John?"

"I'm not sure. I'll send them up after dinner."

"That's good. As happy as I am. I'm also exhausted. I need a nap."

"You sleep. I'll be right here when you wake up. I'm not going anywhere." He leaned over and gave her a gentle kiss. "I love you."

"I love you, too. Forever."

He kissed her again. "And a day."

Lydia smiled. Life couldn't get much sweeter. She was married to the love of her life. The only man she'd ever loved. She had her animal clinic, thanks to Walter, and she had her wonderful children thanks to Max.

Her life was the best it could be, and she was thankful every day.

About the Author

Cynthia Woolf is the award winning and best-selling author of twenty-five historical western romance books and two short stories with more books on the way.

Cynthia loves writing and reading romance. Her first western romance, *Tame A Wild Heart,* was inspired by the story her mother told her of meeting Cynthia's father on a ranch in Creede, Colorado. Although *Tame A Wild Heart* takes place in Creede that is the only similarity between the stories. Her father was a cowboy not a bounty hunter and her mother was a nursemaid (called a nanny now) not the ranch owner. The ranch they met on is still there as part of the open space in Mineral County in southwestern Colorado.

Writing as CA Woolf, she has six sci-fi, space opera romance titles. She calls them westerns in space.

Cynthia credits her wonderfully supportive husband Jim and her critique partners for saving her sanity and allowing her to explore her creativity.

WEBSITE
http://cynthiawoolf.com

NEWSLETTER
https://www.subscribepage.com/k1p2m1

Made in the USA
Coppell, TX
30 November 2021